I0692164

Paul A. Green

The stories and articles in this collection appeared in the Terminal Press anthology *Deep Ends* from 2013 to 2024. 'The Impossibility Exhibition' was originally written for collaboration with video artist Jeremy Welsh while 'Remote Sensing' is the opening sequence from a forthcoming novel. Paul's earlier novels include *The Qliphoth* (Libros Libertad 2007) and *Beneath the Pleasure Zones I & II* (Mandrake of Oxford 2014/2016). His poetry collections include *The Gestaltbunker— Selected Poems* (Shearsman Books 2012), while his audio work can be found on the CD *Sounds and Symbols* (Phantom Airship 2017) and at www.culturecourt.com. A selection of his plays for radio and stage has been published in *Babalon* (Scarlet Imprint 2015). His website is paulgreenwriter.co.uk.

TERMINAL TRANSMISSIONS

PAUL A. GREEN

TERMINAL
PRESS

Terminal Transmissions

ISBN: 978-1-990682-11-7

First Edition

Published By
THE TERMINAL PRESS
Powell River, BC, Canada

The short stories are entirely works of fiction.
All of the characters, organizations, and events portrayed in these stories
are either products of the author's imagination or are used fictitiously. Any
resemblance to actual persons, living or dead (except for satirical purposes), is
entirely coincidental.

Contents

THE
IMPOSSIBILITY
EXHIBITION

ARTISTE

As Jacqueline Mayakovski deftly tacked up yet another rectangle of daubed sugar paper, Dr. Greenhaus speculated idly. Why was this mysterious girl in the paint-stained smock continually putting up these delinquents' paintings, day after day, as if to cover every surface in the building? Perhaps she found this display of motor skills compulsive, yet therapeutic. More likely she was an amnesiac performance artist, stranded in the school long after the expiry of her corporate sponsorship, and now unable ever to face her journey home across the reptile-infested subways of the ruined city. She was smiling enigmatically, like the sun-faded clipping of Brigitte Bardot he'd found pasted inside a staff-room locker; and her lips flickered, as if in synchronisation with some fleeting subliminal impulse. But her comment was drowned in the roar of a Sea King landing in the playground outside, bringing in another contingent of exhausted riot police and bewildered behavioural dysfunction specialists. Everywhere, they were arriving too late. Their clients, an army of proletarian *artistes manqués*, were fleeing the schools in their thousands. As the helicopter settled, whirling vortices of dust and litter were scattered against the chain-links of the playground perimeter fence.

EXHIBIT 2000

Every morning, after a night of uneasy dreams on the broken staffroom furniture, and token breakfast from a vandalised vending machine, he would try to decode the latent content of these infantile artefacts. Jacqueline Mayakovski continued her silent work throughout the night, like a spectral handmaiden of Delvaux gliding through the marble amphitheatres of sleep. Soon she would have decorated every floor of the nine storey building with the pupils' imagery. He wandered among their abstractions, crude spirals of cerise or magenta hanging like deranged miniature galaxies against the grey rectangular geometries of the dinner-room. Upstairs, the walls outside the biology lab were covered in watercolour surreal pastiches, cryptozoic vegetation sprouting a giant penis with a bow tie, an insect-headed woman with a flaming whip. The landscapes of such primal terrors were presumably beyond the reach of the cadres of psychotherapists and social workers who had once filled the school every day. Indeed, despite his own basic training in psychopathology (a hurried crash-course, before his enforced redeployment to the school) Greenhaus was unable to enter the mindscapes of these remedial-room Dalis and Ernsts. The once-prized doctorate in comparative literature that had hung over his desk at All Souls' was little use to him in his role as supply teacher. He should have taken up that option of Communications Consultant with the Mitsoguchi Corporation, but it was too late now.

MEDIA MASTER

In the English Department stockroom, among the piles of burned books, he found a working TV set. As bands of purple cloud darkened around the silhouettes of the gutted office buildings, Greenhaus watched the Headmaster guesting on an early-evening talkshow. "We are bringing them back into the school system," the Head told the studio audience, "and we shall restart the heart of our nation's classrooms with our pedagogic skills, our curriculum- mapping skills, our pastoral management skills. We are waiting to reclaim our youth any day now. It is not an impossible task...." Greenhaus had not seen a pupil for seventeen days and now only a handful of teachers managed to arrive for the staff meetings and case conferences that had once dominated their working day. Those who survived commuting by armoured bus left well before dusk. Many, like the melancholy Traven or the introverted Koestler, had been kidnapped (or killed) by their ex-pupils, who now owed their loyalties to rival groups of local militia, each flaunting its distinctive style of weaponry and sportswear. Greenhaus heard a footstep in the corridor and instinctively reached for his largactil gun. Although its last dart had been discharged long ago, he found its presence reassuring. But the presence on the doorway was Jacqueline Mayakovski, who removed her dark glasses and produced a Luger from under her iridescent plastic raincoat. She held it in both hands, like a female investigator in a re-run of The Rockford Files. He could hear the distant throb of the helicopters. "You're always in the way, Dr Greenhaus. I've waited hours to get access to this room for the Exhibition. You're all making it impossible for us." Calmly she fired, into the heart of the TV set. The Headmaster's face imploded.

THE CATALOGUE OF APOCALYPSE

After their encounter in the English stockroom, Greenhaus saw little of Jacqueline Mayakovski in the days that followed. He imagined she held some private territory of her own, perhaps in the art studios on the fourth floor, where she nurtured edible fungi or cultivated luminous crystals. The security staff had finally withdrawn for the duration and there was no-one else left to challenge their free movement around the building, or indeed question any aspect of their identity. Greenhaus was more preoccupied with the increasing difficulty of finding food in the roach-infested kitchens and with his ongoing attempt to devise a definitive collection of significant artefacts, his own response to the proliferating collage of pictures that covered the interior walls of the building, his uniquely private view. Patrolling the site and picking up litter had always been one of his regular academic duties. Now it was imperative for his psychic survival, a perverse archeology of the future. As he discovered the objects he assembled them in one of the English Department classrooms and spread them across the empty desks, visual aids for a object lesson in his own increasingly fissile consciousness. At the end of the day he itemised them in an old register:

• Fourth-year worksheets on AIDS with bar charts on the spread of HIV infection and comprehension passage on the symptomatic presentation of Kaposi's sarcoma.

• Video cassette of *The Slow Learning*, presumably a tape used in teacher training.

• Broken surveillance camera, torn from the lobby in a recent incident with intruders.

• Torn copy of *Sunday Sport*, headline: "Schoolgirls' six-in-a-bed sex romp with Sir!".

• Life-size papier-mache effigy of Salman Rushdie, made by

Wahidur Ali, 5P with pins protruding and extensive scorch-marks.

• Star 'Vaders pocket electronic game— "Destroy Earth in order to save it!"

• Audio cassette—"Chaos Pathworking Tape—gives keys and formulae for tapping into Voidflow of Infinite Potential..."

• Polaroid snap of Jacqueline Mayakovski, in deep trance, scraping particles of clay off a potter's wheel, possibly a promotional photo for the school's creative arts course, more likely part of the documentation of a long-term time-based art activity.

• Broken twelve-inch single: Style Assessment by the Quantum Brothers—the Terminal (Death House) Mix.

• EEG records of staff alpha and theta rhythms in simulated stress situations.

• Tissue samples, in vitro, labelled "Left hemisphere, Wernicke's area, a typical fourteen year old."

• Designs for cosmetically effective "client-friendly" CS gasmasks, abandoned, for budgetary reasons, at the testing stage.

• Confidential minutes of a staff disciplinary hearing: "Dr. G's mood-swings giving rise to profound anxieties at the pastoral/pupil interface level".

RED ALERT

The classroom was empty, like a drained swimming-pool. However, although the effort of scouring the overturned filing-cabinets in the Headmaster's office had exhausted Greenhaus, he still stood for a full fifty-five minutes at the front of the darkening room, shouting at the overturned chairs and tables, as if trying to admonish a gang of escaping poltergeists. Despite himself, it was impossible to stop his anxiety ritual of teaching. The rigid templates of the timetable had been etched into his fragile spinal geometry over years, maybe decades, in the industry. His neural warning systems had been on full alert for so long that he could not remember a time when he hadn't spent most of his waking hours pre-empting hostile missile attacks or intervening in minor tribal conflicts. The blank cuboid geometry of the room, its insolent void of wired glass and grubby melamine, might , even now, conceal some vindictive prank learned from Ulster or Vietnam, a sticky membrane of Semtex under a pile of folders, a poisoned thumb-tack on the teacher's chair. He groped for the edge of the graffiti-gouged chalkboard, his pitted lips twitching, his arms waving in the familiar rhythms of exhortation and rebuke, his ears already roaring with the white noise of rioting adolescent mobs, his vision a reddish mist of primal fury. It was his responsibility to preserve world peace. But this was a crisis of the cerebellum, the deep brain, the saurian guardian of his most secret uterine territories, the Mezozoic realms of his Id. His adrenalin overload would rush him down the time-corridors to press the red button, to unleash the purifying radiation of his submerged megatons, those ultimate global peacemakers, which alone could bring him the primaeval silence he craved, the infinite silence of archeopsychic time. That would teach them a lesson.

MADONNA OF THE SUBURBS

When, hours later, he awoke from the sudden fugue, he found himself sprawled on the floor, hands around the charred throat of the Rushdie effigy, which was already crumbling into fragments like a ravaged mummy. The firedrill alarm was still buzzing, a high-pitched sine-wave undulating as monotonously as a line of man-made concrete dunes on a weapons-testing range. Jacqueline Mayakovski stood over him with a cup of black coffee and an apple. Her long iridescent coat hung from her shoulders like the plumage of an exotic bird. "You're getting carried away again, Dr. Greenhaus." She knelt and studied the sutures of his skull with clinical calm. "These fantasies of cosmic destruction and re-creation are all in your head." She had the bright but firm manner of a young mother confronting a wayward toddler in its first Freudian excesses. "You're suffering from iconic overdose, Doctor. It's just one of the symptoms. If you'd had to study those children's pictures for months on end, as I have, you might begin to understand the whole syndrome. You'd better hurry up, before I start taking the exhibition down." She raised the coffee cup to his lips and glided away. He could imagine her now as a housewife in the lost paradises of the leafy suburbs, guiding anima of Botticellian garden-parties, an enigmatic madonna smiling down from the balconies of memory.

THE TERMINAL REPORTS

In the evenings, as he sat in the physics labs on the sixth floor, the signals from hundreds of orbiting TV satellites penetrating every tissue of his body, Greenhaus was sometimes tempted to pick up his infra-red binoculars and scan the tower blocks on the far side of the motorway. He hoped to see someone watching alien porn, some ghostly conjunction of limbs as distant and implausible as the docking of Iraqi and Iranian space modules. But tonight, as every night, he only glimpsed the dark outline of satellite dishes, tiny excrescent fungi sprouting above blank windows and empty walkways. Soon he was overcome by his other obsessive urge, to complete his terminal reports, a task as huge (and seemingly futile) as Jacqueline Mayakovski's exhibition, curated for pupils and parents who had long ago turned their backs on the static hand-made artefact to participate in the ever-shifting continuum of an exploding electronic universe. A few lights flickered in the towers, like cave-fires in a cliff-face of the night. He tried to ignore their allure as he thumbed through the interleaved carbons of the report forms and attempted to find convincing formulae to explain the increasing inability of the species to educate its offspring. "Lack of attention..violently disruptive behaviour...an habitual non-attender..."—the ready-made phrases in boxes, designed for faster ticking and a rationalised assessment procedure, no longer made sense, for clients whose hyper-fast senses were unsystematically deranged. They had long since taken the extra-mural option. The rumble of distant explosions and the distorted blare of sound systems on the night wind disturbed his concentration. The actual topology of the laboratory, its cage-like enclosure of space, was contracting around him, as if the gravity of his presence was warping the flickering fluorescent light. He had to move from this constricting spatio-temporal matrix. As he left, in search of Jacqueline Mayakovski and her Sybilline folios, he tossed the report forms into a wastebin and added a lighted match.

THE IMPOSSIBILITY EXHIBITION

"You see, Doctor, the pictures regress as the pupils get older." Jacqueline Mayakovski sat among the Rousseauesque jungle of her potted plants and sifted through the piles of pictures. "Here is a standard third-year fantasy." She pointed to one of the pseudo-surrealist gouaches that Greenhaus had noticed outside the Life Science room. In a burning desert, under orange skies, a squat headless earth-coloured hermaphrodite was being eaten by a robotic crustacean. The picture was entitled "Deathworld—James Tallis 3B." "That's just apocalyptic mannerism, I realise," she added, half-apologetically, "but compare it to what last year's fifth year were doing." The wall behind her was papered with torn sheets covered in wild scrawls, gestural spray-gun marks, a demented calligraphy that seemed compelled to cross a given space with as many savage loops and violent intersections as possible, as if that were the only way it could trace and affirm its actuality, in a polymorphous-perverse act of self-obliteration. "It's not just like the territorial death-tags on the subways," she said, with a faint shudder. Greenhaus recalled how travellers sometimes blundered into inner-city free-fire zones, often dying horribly, simply because they couldn't read such sinister tribal glyphs. "This is a unique collection of autographs, by a generation of autists. I'm not an intellectual, Doctor. I'll leave the rest of the explanations to you." She made for the door. He tried to follow, but her sure-footed agility had already taken her up the first turn of the darkened stairwell. His route also went upwards, through the smoke-filled corridors, where he lost her.

TERMINAL EXHIBITIONIST

"An electron, " shouted Dr. Greenhaus, to the masses far below, "is a photonic system trapped in a space-time cavity..." Police searchlight beams stabbed the night sky. A rising wind was blowing bitterly up here on the roof of the school and he doubted if the young bodies pressed against the mesh of the playground fence could hear a word. The cheap megaphone was already filtering and processing his utterance, turning him into a mere transient sample in an acid-house mix-down. In any case, he was certain that the crowd had been drawn by huge tongues of flame, now licking the windows of the labs, under the impression this was the work of their peers. They were chanting unintelligibly and surging against the wire, as firemen began to run a hydraulic hoist up the sheer glass side of the building. Policemen with perspex shields glinting in the firelight formed a hollow square around the edge of the playground. A smaller group of officers—marksmen, trained negotiators?—were waving him down. He gripped the side of a ventilation duct and began to hurl textbooks into the darkness; but it was a futile display. It was only a matter of time as to who would get to him first, the kids or the Educational Security forces. Both extrapolations were negative. He had only minutes to finish his exposition.

TIME-WINDOWS (1)

Greenhaus threw away the megaphone and lifted a pocket cassette machine to his lips. Despite the increasing noise and smoke, he was determined to file his last report from the terminal zone. "The students' "paintings" are not merely the expression of anomie or socio-economic malaise. They are the semiotics of a mutant ontology, an autistic withdrawal from the physical constraints of Newtonian time and causality. Faced with the conflicting claims of "reality" and the "virtual reality" of the electronic media landscape, with the bewildering seductions of hyper-possibility, in which even the simplest of our actions creates an unpredictable wave-front of improbability, they are seeking relief in atavism." He crouched on the flat asphalt roof, shouting into the tiny microphone while the great rotors of the Sea King throbbed overhead. "For, as they accelerate along the time-gradient of adolescence towards adulthood, they feel increasingly trapped in the black hole of their own body-identities. The continuum folds back in on them, like the roof of a sabotaged aircraft. Matter itself is a time-trap."

TIME-WINDOWS (2)

As armed Ed Sec officers leaped from the hatch of the Sea King, Greenhaus wondered if Jacqueline Mayakovski had escaped the multi-storey inferno. He could not help feeling admiration and even affection for this serene self-possessed young woman, who had survived the horrors of the recent months with such grace and aplomb. He wished he'd paid greater attention during her earlier conversational gambits, about everyday hobbies like cycling or swimming or handicrafts. A gun barrel prodded his left pectoral. He didn't resist as two burly Australian Ed Sec orderlies grabbed his arms, while a thin lizard-faced medic searched for a vein in his scabbed flesh. As the needle sank in, the gannet-like screaming of the children slowly faded like a huge panoramic sweep of white noise; and the whine of the helicopter turbines sank to a diminuendo. He looked up. It was almost dawn. Light was breaking against the black towers, bursting through the terraced citadels of indigo cloud, and against the light he could perceive motion, avian movement, the beat of angelic wings. In her flimsy hand-made craft of paper and wood, the ornithoptric bird-woman of the art room was rising on the thermals of the burning school, far above the all-consuming flames of the Impossibility Exhibition, towards her reborn paradises in the forests of the South.

The WATCH TOWERS

JG Ballard liked "The Watch-Towers." Indeed, it was one of his favourites, as David Pringle has discovered from some notes the author had written to his Italian translator in 1967. It is certainly one that I've returned to again and again over the years, mesmerised by its fusion of bourgeois paranoia and apocalyptic menace. Ballard, in those same notes, stated that it came to him 'in a dream', and in its quiet way the story is as surreal as anything he ever wrote. It is perhaps Magritte, rather than Dali—in ways I will return to later.

I suspect it also reprises specific aspects of his Lungwha experience and his subsequent encounter with the environment and life-style of post-war austerity England. Although the story was published in June 1962 in *Science Fantasy*, for me it vividly evokes the ambience of 1950s Home Counties subtopia. I grew up in Wimbledon, a few miles up the commuter rail link to Shepperton and my father worked stoically in the bureaucracy of local government, so reading "The Watch-Towers" triggers a certain sepia-toned nostalgia, an emotion which the auteur himself greatly distrusted, haunted as he was by darker images from his own past.

And, of course, there's the enigma of the Towers themselves. Blogger Tom Moody, reading the piece through the lens of traditional sf tropes, praises it as 'one of the best alien invasion stories' (although there's no explicit reference to an extraterrestrial threat) while a Freudian reader like Sam Francis might see these mysterious erections as surrogate phalli, each one hanging in permanent inverted suspension like some sexualised sword of Damocles. Are they an externalisation of Cold War angst about nuclear missiles, a constant looming threat? Or are they foreshadowings of our global surveillance culture? The Towers are polysemic, they become floating signifiers hovering over the desolation of our dreamscapes...

To explore the significance of the Towers in the text of the story and the context of the writer's life, it's probably simplest to take a linear walk through the narrative. Like so many Ballard stories, it begins with a back-story that is quickly established, presenting a subversion of consensus reality as a *fait accompli*. The Watch-Towers are already in place, suspended in geometrical formation over the crumbling rooftops and shabby denizens of this anonymous suburb; and there's a flurry of activity behind their windows as protagonist Renthall sets off from his cheap hotel for his liaison with Mrs Osmond. 'Optical equipment' is being adjusted. An elderly man outside the library tells Renthall that they're 'up to something…'

At one level, there's perhaps an implied parallel with the twitching of net curtains at the sight of a potential adulterer, motivated by a combination of prim disapproval and voyeuristic envy. But at a deeper level, permeating the whole story, is the motif of overall surveillance by a potentially hostile agency or entity, and the nervous appeasement of the local authority, the Council.

We cannot forget that Ballard spent three formative years of his life being watched—from guard towers, sentry boxes, perimeter fences, in roll-calls and night patrols. Throughout his entire internment his elders in their various committees anxiously studied the behaviour of their captors, trying to anticipate what instructions the camp commander might have received about their ultimate fate. From *Miracles of Life* we learn that the last few months in Lungua were especially fraught with insecurity as the Japanese regime collapsed around them. Although there are many models for the literature of paranoia, most notably in Kafka, I'm convinced that the paranoid undertone in the piece—a deep sub-sonic—emanates from the Lunghua years.

Renthall cautiously makes his way to Mrs Osmond's house through streets of empty semi-derelict houses (vistas of post-war English Settlement in Shanghai and/or the bombed-out streets of London) for an assignation that is tentative and repressed as a scene from *Brief Encounter*.

One imagines Julia Osmond as a 40s/50s British Gaumont star, bleached and buxom like Diana Dors but with a RP accent like Glynis Johns or Kay Kendall. There's a hint of sensuality in her 'plump hips' but it is kept in check by her fears that the Towers are watching. She's aware of Renthall's sexual potential and even laughs ironically about it, but fornication in the suburbs, a staple of mainstream 'literary fiction', is overshadowed (literally) by the presence of the Towers. Their dialogue is desultory, establishing that the school where Renthall used to teach is still closed. School closure was one of the punitive sanctions used by the camp commander during the final phase of Lungua.

As a gift Renthall brings Julia a tattered woman's magazine—a rare item of barter in the scavenger economy of the camp. He also invites his mistress to another cultural activity enjoyed by internees, a classical musical recital, on gramophone records. But, like the camp inmates, Julia has heard these crackly 78 rpm discs of Greig and Tchaikovski too often. Predictably she also rejects Renthall's wary advances, so that he leaves, frustrated by her inertia and lassitude, which she shares with the rest of this isolated micro-community, all over-awed by their mysterious Panopticon.

When Renthall's teaching colleague Hanson informs him that the Council disapproves of his affair, he is outraged by this intrusion into his privacy, but Hanson warns him that it might be prudent to 'take our cue'—a typically British evasive phrase— from the municipal authorities who might even be in contact with the Towers. There's an ongoing subtext that the sudden spike of activity on the viewing decks is somehow related to Renthall's sexual involvement with Julia (who shares her name with the female protagonist of Orwell's *Nineteen Eighty-Four*).

Learning that the local cinema is also going to be closed, as the Council takes on the attributes of a puritanical 'Watch Committee', Renthall decides to rebel. His act of subversion is not to occupy the Town Hall or organise demos to challenge the Council bye-law that forbids assemblies in the street. Instead, he proposes to organise a garden fête…

There's a pleasingly absurdist element in this, for the garden fête seems a quintessentially conservative, even Tory institution, typical of suburban Shepperton, a Conservative seat since 1950. Yet public festivity can become a statement of defiance, as Renthall points out to an apprehensive Hanson, a focus of communal celebration that might awaken the citizens from their lethargy. Their fatalism has much in common with the post-war exhaustion and defeatism that so depressed the young Jim Ballard when he arrived in England in 1946.

And Renthall himself is beset by anxiety and irrational guilt. On a second visit to a more animated Mrs Osmond, he admits to a crisis of confidence over his obsession with the Towers and seems to ignore her 'cool fingers' in his hair. They are both trapped in an emotional impasse, in a static relationship like the social microcosm around them.

Renthall's proposition makes people uneasy—even Doctor Clifton, whom he respects for not slumping into the general apathy that has gripped the rest of the community. His eventual ally in the fête enterprise is a typical figure from early postwar Britain: the spiv, a cigar-chewing hustler and pimp in a broad check overcoat, Boardman, the cinema owner. Boardman, a precursor perhaps of another more sinister entrepreneur, Strangman in *The Drowned World*, has his own agenda for collaborating with Renthall and offers him the use of a beer-garden directly under the gaze of a Watch Tower.

At this point, it's worth considering the visual details of the Towers themselves. They hover in geometrical formation in a bluish haze, an overcast which obscures the horizon and the upper atmosphere, concealing their origin and effectively isolating the world they survey.

They appear to be metallic, although Renthall can't see traces of rivets or welding. And, curiously, they are rectangular rather than cylindrical, which might suggest the author wasn't overtly deploying Freudian symbolism in the text. They are like 'rectangular chimneys over an industrial landscape, wreathed in white smoke.' One is reminded of various surrealist paintings, notably by Magritte, which feature huge objects suspended in a cloudscape. *The Castle of the Pyrenees* depicts a gigantic rock with a castle at its apex, suspended against a blue sky. Admittedly, it's over a seascape, but the sense of menace and oppression is palpable.

Another painting, *La Carte D'Après Nature*, displays enormous rectangular blocks hanging in the clouds over a ruined house. I am not suggesting that those specific paintings had any direct influence on the story. But Ballard had been immersed in surrealist art since he was a schoolboy and the skies of Dali and Magritte, populated by vast objects wrenched from their normal contexts, might have contributed to creating the cyclorama of his dreams. "The Watch-Towers" is perhaps one of the pictures that Ballard might have aspired to paint if he had developed Dalinian technical skills.

Renthall is soon visited by a Council bureaucrat, Barnes, who predictably requests him to cancel the fête, implying there is a direct chain of command between the Council and the Towers. Renthall refuses and therefore is summoned to attend a Council committee meeting the following day. Mrs Osmond believes that his anxieties about this encounter are groundless. She feels the Council has a permissive tolerance of their affair and that he has developed an exaggerated notion of his own significance.

When Renthall learns the meeting has been cancelled, he feels vindicated. The authority of the Council via their alleged relationship with the Towers has been challenged and they are already in retreat. Yet, as he informs Mulvaney, the hotel manager, of his triumph, the ground of the narrative begins to shift. For when he asks Mulvaney if he has noticed any new activity 'out there', referring to the nearest Tower, the manager seems puzzled.

Soon Renthall feels frustrated at losing the opportunity to confront the Council in person. He also feels uneasy, realising that the Council might have simply stood aside to let the Towers respond to his insubordination, which, he rationalises, was surely only a token gesture. Meanwhile Mulvaney has ordered the construction of a sun-bathing platform on the roof of the hotel, in full view of the Towers while Boardman has constructed a complete fun fair in the beer garden, with Hanson's enthusiastic support. Renthall is worried that will be reprisals, and that the Council is simply biding its time before taking action. Yet people seem indifferent to the Towers now and are slightly non-plussed by his references to them.

This shift in consensus reality becomes even more pronounced when Renthall turns to Dr Clifton for validation. He insists that a process of mass hypnosis has begun, whereby people can no longer see the Towers. The Doctor-figure, encountered often in Ballard, exemplified by Dr Ransome in

Empire of the Sun, is frequently benevolent, a saviour or mentor. Here Dr. Clifton is non-committal, humours Renthall's apparent fantasy and gives him sleeping tablets.

The school has re-opened but Renthall doesn't return. As the sidewalk cafe fills up and Boardman's fun palace is in full swing, he calls on Mrs Osmond, determined to confront her directly and test his precarious sanity. But she cannot see the Towers from her garden, she cannot even recall their existence and is bewildered by Renthall's agitated questioning. He reminds her that they used to draw the curtains when they were upstairs together. With characteristic middle-class notions of propriety, she protests that the neighbours will hear...

He flees towards the deserted outskirts of the town, the Towers still visible 'like a continuous palisade' around it. The old man he met outside the library is absent-mindedly scanning the sky, but he runs on into a patch of wasteland. Then the whole

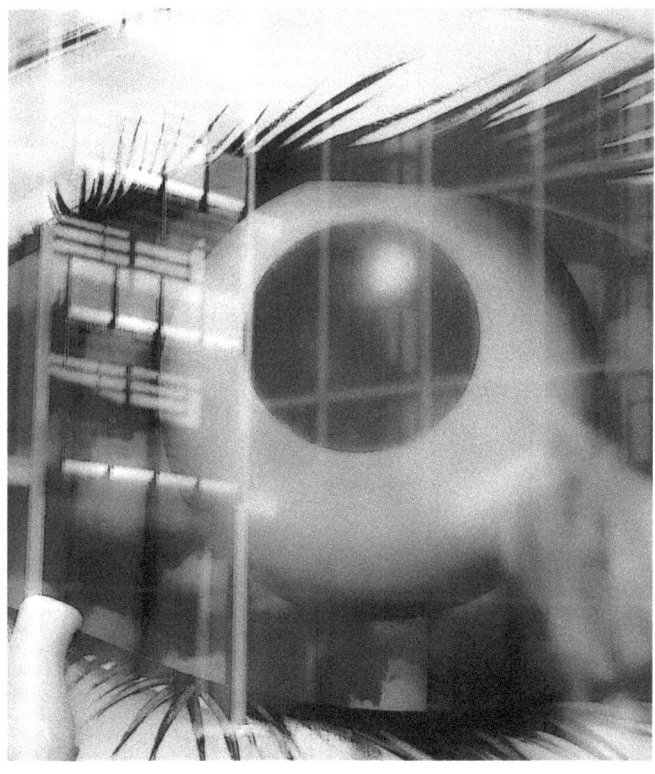

sky 'sparkled as if the air was opening and shutting.' The haze has dissipated and the observation windows in the Towers are wide-open, allowing the watchers to gaze down on him…

The enigma of this ending, with its multiplicity of connotations, has been enriched by subsequent events in the life-world. The 'optical equipment' of the Towers is now fibre-optical, allegedly allowing GCHQ to deploy 'Optic Nerve' and study our personal relationships as mediated by web-cam, a technology anticipated by Ballard in "The Intensive Care Unit."

And if I decided to organise a Ballardian garden fête in Shepperton—perhaps a re-enactment of one of the idyllic scenes from *The Unlimited Dream Company*—the National Security Agency would have no problem accessing the guest list or even infiltrating a virtual guest on to the Facebook page, should they consider this to be a subversive gathering, a potential target for the spy cams of a drone.

The UK, that country young Ballard found so alien and censorious, now has more CCTV cameras and bored security men staring at screens than any other country in the world; and the industrialisation of voyeurism via the internet has created millions more watchers, justifying Ballard's famous quote that 'sex multiplied by technology equals the future.'

These days Renthall might never get as far as actually meeting Mrs Osmond. Typing 'plump blonde middle class mature' into Google might be enough to satisfy his dreams, an action duly recorded, of course, by his service provider and trackable in real time via the latest digital advertising technology.

The Towers are always on watch.

Staring Down the Eye of the Cyclone
The Wind From Nowhere

On the night of October 15 1987 my wife, already a Ballard admirer, began reading *The Wind from Nowhere* for the first time. As we retired to bed in our suburban London apartment, the whine of the wind, which had been rising all evening, became a sustained scream and continued for hours. The sound both terrified and exhilarated us, as if we'd somehow evoked it by reading the book, with its powerful descriptions of the pulverisation of our familiar cityscape. Yet we were absurdly confident that our modern block would survive undamaged, which indeed it did, despite the winds of up to 100 mph that swept through south-east England.

In the morning, of course, we learned how the Great Storm had caused deaths and massive destruction across the region. But for us it had briefly resembled what Brian Aldiss in *Billion Year Spree* called 'a cosy catastrophe', referring to the British disaster novels of the 1950s, like John Wyndham's *Day of the Triffids*. Here the reader enjoys the voyeuristic *jouissance* of witnessing cataclysmic destruction and the reassuring *plaisir* of seeing civilisation restored through British pluck and grit.

The themes of catastrophe and the destruction of all mankind's works are embedded in ancient mythology and religion, notably the Epic of Gilgamesh and Old Testament narratives of flood or apocalypse. They emerge in speculative fiction and scientific romance throughout the nineteenth and early twentieth century, exemplified by Edgar Allen Poe's *The Conversation of Eiros and Charmion* (1839), in which a passing comet poisons the Earth's atmosphere and M.P Shiel's *The Purple Cloud* (1901). A noxious gas escapes from the Earth's crust and kills off all humanity, except the hero and the Eve figure he eventually discovers. As the genre evolves, the possibilities of cosmic or environmental menace are explored with ever greater ingenuity. In Richard Matheson's *The Last Day* (1953) the sun goes nova while in Philip Latham's *The Xi Effect* (1950) a localised space-time distortion causes the Earth to contract in relation to the wavelength of light, leaving the human race plunged into total darkness and panic.

The Wind from Nowhere follows this trajectory, in that the global hurricane is caused by phenomena that are entirely indifferent to human concerns and are not even anthropogenic. Whereas the catastrophe of *The Drought* is caused by industrial waste disrupting the natural evaporation cycles of the world's oceans, the cataclysms of *The Wind from Nowhere*, *The Drowned World*, *The Crystal World* and *The Voices of Time* are the side-effects of vast impersonal environmental or cosmic processes. At his core, Ballard is an existentialist, keenly aware that any meaning in existence is created in defiance of an indifferent cosmos. As he stated in an essay on 'Cataclysms and Dooms' in *The Visual Encyclopaedia of Science Fiction* (1977):

> 'I believe that the catastrophe story, whoever may tell it, represents a constructive and positive act by the imagination rather than a negative one, an attempt to confront the terrifying void of a patently meaningless universe by challenging it at its own game, to remake zero by provoking it in every conceivable way.'

The story concept of *The Wind from Nowhere* is perhaps a challenge to orthodox science, attributing the cause of the wind to 'a vast tangential stream of cosmic radiation.' Its gravitational drag, according to a government meteorologist, 'might have set in motion the huge cyclone revolving round the Earth's axis.' This is no more or less absurd than the inciting incident in the 1961 British disaster movie *The Day the Earth Caught Fire*, in which the simultaneous testing of giant nuclear weapons by the USA and the Soviet Union causes the Earth to drift off its orbit towards the sun. Here mankind's own follies are the catalyst for potential calamity. Like the classic British disaster novels of the fifties, the film acts out Cold War anxieties about nuclear holocaust and demonstrates how the supposed British middle class capacity for keeping calm and carrying on might enable us to cope with social disruption and contemplate possible annihilation. Works like John Christopher's *The Death of Grass* begin with similarly speculative extrapolations and explore—more pessimistically—our capacity for sustaining civilisation in the face of global famine. But as Christopher Daly (2013) points out:

> While Ballard's catastrophes significantly distort the formula of the genre, they also mark another step in its historical development that had already seen a transformation from Wyndham's 'cosy' narratives to Christopher's supposedly 'semi-cosy' fictions. Ballard's success in radicalising the form is found in his willingness to move beyond the linear structure of preceding British catastrophe novels—which largely follow the pattern of pre-apocalyptic order, followed by catastrophe before reaching an ultimately hopeful post-apocalyptic order—and analyse instead the unspoken, latent energies that continually prompt narratives of catastrophe.

The Wind from Nowhere certainly has its antecedents, but as we shall see, it also foreshadows distinctive tropes in Ballard's writing, both in the disaster novels and in the subsequent work. Although it is tempting to see *The Wind from Nowhere* as part of an 'elemental quartet' , in which it explores the realm of Air, while the others deal with Fire, Water, and Earth, this 'alchemical' reading of Ballard, however it might resonate at an archetypal level, doesn't appear to correspond with any overtly mystical aspirations on his behalf.

Ballard famously excluded the book from his official *oeuvre*, dismissing it as 'my one piece of out and out commercial fiction' that had been written during a two week holiday to launch him as a Berkley Books author in the US market. One can't help seeing this in mythic terms, rather like the mystique surrounding Jack Kerouac's three-week typing marathon that produced the scroll of *On the Road*, which was actually composed with the aid of numerous notebooks and then subsequently heavily edited. In Ballard's case, he was developing a story that had appeared in two instalments as 'Storm Wind' in *New Worlds* (September and October 1961) which gave him opportunities for revision.

David Pringle has noted that that he removed references in the opening paragraphs to Gravesend, Wapping, Esher and other British locations which might have confused his American readers. He also cut an epilogue set in Iceland, after the wind has dropped, where a farmer and his family discover a cache of tinned food—a scene probably inspired by memories of the food parcels parachuted from American planes over Lunghua camp in August 1945. I suspect the underlying reason for Ballard's repudiation of his first novel is that it represented a regression, both stylistically and conceptually, from the sophistication of some of his earlier short stories, notably 'The Voices of Time', published in *New Worlds* in 1960 and the various *Vermilion Sands* pieces that had appeared in *Science Fantasy*. He admitted to David Pringle in a 1975 interview: 'I was tempted to approach it seriously. I mean, it could have been done on a completely serious level—by serious I mean on the level of the other novels, *The Drowned World* and so forth—and I nearly did do it that way. I don't know whether it would have been any better, because the wind thing isn't that interesting. So I thought I'd use all the clichés there are, the standard narrative conventions, and I sat down at the typewriter and I wrote the book...'

The book certainly works (for the most part) as a straightforward adventure narrative. It also demonstrates Ballard's strong visual imagination in evoking apocalyptic scenes and tentatively probes the motivations of his characters as they respond to their predicament. Its sub-texts reveal some of the underlying social tensions of its time as well as Ballard's recurrent obsessions. One might argue that it was a necessary stage in his development, not only in career terms, but in giving him the challenge of integrating the generic demands of a multi-strand action-driven scenario with the possibilities of exploring inner spaces and doomscapes.

The first chapter introduces Dr Donald Maitland, one of Ballard's many doctor figures and one of his three Maitlands (Richard in 'Gioconda of the Twilight Noon' and Robert in *Concrete Island*) who has attempted, in vain, to board his flight from Heathrow to Vancouver. Like all other flights it has been cancelled due to excessively high winds. As he makes his way back through windswept London he notices the fine silicate dust that is coating every surface, the first indication of the erosion of the Earth's wind-blown top soil—and a prefiguring of the dunescapes that recur so frequently in the Ballardian world. Maitland, who is trying to separate from his errant wife Susan, a wealthy trustafarian neurotic, is already the typical Ballardian observer. He is now emotionally disengaged after her serial infidelities, most recently with an aspiring racing driver. It might be far-fetched to suggest that Peter Sylvester, whom Maitland encounters when he returns to his flat, is a precursor of Seagrave in *Crash*. But Grand Prix drivers like Mike Hawthorne and Stirling Moss were acquiring celebrity status in the late nineteen-fifties and the inclusion of Sylvester is a deft way of signposting Susan's preferred milieu, a fragile world in which glamour and social rank are soon to be endangered.

The increasing menace of the wind is vividly reinforced when Maitland leaves Susan to stay with his friend Symington. His taxi driver is electrocuted by a falling power cable that 'flailed across him like an enormous phosphorescent lash' while radio bulletins report hurricanes across the Equator and the Far East. Symington, a government employee, tells him that the brown dust is topsoil blown from Tibet and that the government is taking 'precautionary moves' to prepare 'at least a handful of deep shelters.' Symington continues: 'As long as one tenth of one per cent of the population is catered for, everybody's happy... But God help the other 99.9.'

As this first strand in the novel develops, following Maitland's involvement with the British establishment's attempt to cope with the crisis, the episodes and images recycle our collective myths and traumas of the Second World War. Sandbagged Admiralty buildings, in which Maitland is co-opted to join Symington in government emergency planning, play host to crisis talks in which officialdom struggles to comprehend what is happening. An early incident, the collapse of the Russell Hotel into the Piccadilly Line underground station where hundreds are sheltering, recalls similar wartime tragedies at Balham and Bethnal Green Tube stations and abiding British folk memories of the Blitz. Ballard vividly describes the desperate attempts of emergency services to rescue people from collapsing buildings and deliver aid across the impassable city. In scenes that perhaps conflate the mythology of WW2 with memories of Lunghua he evokes the dirt and chaos of the overcrowded platforms and the huddled citizens 'walling off crude cubicles with blankets and raincoats, cooking over primus stoves, queueing endlessly at the latrines…' For Maitland, the military men on the committee 'had already been defeated and were ready to make a triumph of it, counting up the endless casualty lists, the catalogues of disaster and destruction, as if these were a measure of their courage and competence.' Maybe the entire sub-genre of post WW2 British disaster novels could be read as a response to the insecurities of post-imperial decline. Certainly, as Maitland and colleagues make their way through the disaster area they pass locations of obvious symbolic significance:

> Nelson's Column was down. Two weeks earlier, when the wind had reached ninety-five mph, a crack which had passed unnoticed for seventy-five years suddenly revealed itself a third of the way up the shaft. The next day the upper section had toppled, the shattered cylindrical segments still lying where they had fallen among the four bronze lions.

But as one might expect, Ballard introduces a Churchillian figure, Simon Marshall, 'a large powerful man of fifty' who is determined to raise morale and insists that Londoners should 'stand up and face this wind together'. One could visualise Marshall being played by Jack Hawkins or Harry Andrews, stars of British nineteen-fifties war movies, stern but charismatic authority figures. However when Maitland visits Marshall's fortified London home and discovers weapons and paramilitary uniforms, he realises that Marshall may have entered a public/ private partnership with the industrialist Hardoon that is ultimately focused on preserving the lives of a ruling elite. Indeed, anxieties about the aftermath of a Third World War are a key sub-text throughout the book. The Campaign for Nuclear

Disarmament (which Ballard later criticised as a 'millenic cult') had been founded in 1958 and had drawn the attention of an angry public to the network of bunkers that the government was building across the country to protect key officials and politicians in the event of a Soviet nuclear attack.

As the storm, now approaching 180 mph, tears the fabric of London apart Marshall's team surveys the devastation via CCTV from a USAF command bunker. In a memorable sequence, Maitland watches helplessly as people try to escape their overcrowded tunnels.

> Like petals torn from a wind-blown flower they detached themselves from the doorways, took a few helpless steps out into the street, and were whipped off their feet and hurled across the road, bouncing head over heels like sacks of feathers that burst and disintegrated as they ripped into the ragged teeth of reinforcing bars protruding from the debris.

The passage has a curious contemporary feel, not only in its brutal imagery but in the way the horror is already mediated via television cameras, like the Youtube video of a terrorist atrocity.

Equally striking is the earlier account of Susan Maitland's death. Maitland has returned to her wrecked apartment in up-market Belgravia, hoping she can be persuaded to take refuge in the tunnels. Like the elegant and capricious Beatrice Dahl of *The Drowned World*, marooned in her penthouse hotel suite, Susan, in her grimy cocktail dress, will not be moved—and embraces the disaster. But whereas Beatrice surrenders to dream and reverie, accepting the gradual metamorphoses in her environment and her psyche, Susan's response is suicidal defiance, a nihilistic thrill-seeking. 'I've been frightened for too long, Donald. Of Daddy and you and myself.' She deliberately allows the wind to catch her:

> Down on his knees Maitland saw her for an instant, catapulted through the updraft rising

from the street, bounce off the roof of the Embassy building and then spin away like a smashed doll into the maze of rooftops beyond. A few feet away the air pounded at the door frames, ripping away the masonry from the exposed edge.

The kinetics of Susan's death are a ghastly parody of human flight—but far from the flight-fantasy of *The Unlimited Dream Company*. She becomes dehumanised, a tiny fragment in a vortex of flying rubble, a Bellmer doll torn apart in a surreal whirlwind. Not long after, Maitland is trapped when his emergency tunnel is blocked by the collapse of a fashionable Knightsbridge department store—but is later conveniently rescued to join the European strand of the narrative.

The European storyline features Lanyon, an American submarine commander, Patricia, an NBC journalist and various extras as they make a dangerous cross-country journey from Genoa to Nice and back, to rescue an American presidential candidate—who is, in fact, already dead. On the outward journey in their armoured car, they help to save lives in a ruined church. On their return trip with the coffin their vehicle is wrecked and they are forced to seek refuge in a monastery on the outskirts of Genoa, where they encounter a gang of looters stockpiling household appliances in the hope of a post-apocalypse consumer boom. There are fisticuffs and

a shoot-out, but when the boss looter recognises Lanyon as the man who saved his wife in the church, he relents. Thus Lanyon and Patricia, who have by now discovered a mutual attraction, are led through a network of tunnels and sewers to the port, and eventually manage to make their way back to the submarine pens. Here Lanyon is tasked to head for the UK, where eventually he and Patricia will meet Maitland.

The challenges of the storm-ravaged terrain and the perils of seeking shelter are competently described. Although the monastery, which is located in the side of a cliff-face, doesn't appear to correspond directly with any monastic buildings in the Genoa area, it's possible that Ballard drew on memories of a European holiday in the 1940s to create a convincing picture of the devastated city and its environs. However the whole strand is the most formulaic element in the novel. One wonders if Ballard felt pressure to add a conventional Hollywood-style love interest and some tough-guy heroics and/or a need to expand the story over two editions of *New Worlds*. After the powerful depictions of destruction and terror in London, the European plot line seems superfluous.

Indeed, when the UK thread is resumed in Chapter Six, 'Death in a Bunker', the book gathers both momentum and resonance. The chapter title recalls another scenario from the mythos of the Second World War, the suicide of Hitler in his Berlin bunker; while death in a post World War Three nuclear bunker was a recurring motif in 1950s SF, notably in Mordecai

36

Roshwald's 1959 novel *Level 7*. The bunker is perhaps the defining architectural structure of the twentieth century just as the Gothic cathedral was of the fourteenth. It is, to quote a 1971 poem of mine, "The Gestaltbunker" where we finally encounter the sum total of our unconscious aspirations as a culture.

Marshall's London bunker is now vulnerable, so attempting to direct rescue operations has become futile. He decides to move out with his PA/mistress Deborah, Maitland's friend Symington and a small skeleton staff. Ostensibly they will travel in a massive tracked vehicle to the US nuclear bunker at Brandon Hall, but it quickly becomes clear from Marshall's furtive scrambled phone calls that he has a prior arrangement with the mysterious industrialist Hardoon, who is supposedly offering him refuge at 'Hardoon Tower'. However, to Deborah's dismay the arrangement doesn't include Symington or the other three support staff—as is made clear when Hardoon's security chief Kroll arrives. His black plastic storm-suit and fibre-glass helmet, reminiscent of the guards at Winnerden Flats in Nigel Kneale's *Quatermass 2*, carry totalitarian connotations, as does his brutal treatment of Marshall's party, now that the director of operations has outlived his usefulness as a supplier of arms and insider informati.on. Despite Marshall's attempts at negotiation his staff are shot dead, Deborah is raped before being killed and Symington is wounded and left for dead. Finally Marshall himself is shot and fatally wounded, although his lingering death in the empty bunker allows him time to send out a distress call on Symington's behalf while contemplating the last functioning CCTV transmission. 'Only one picture was being transmitted now, a white blur of flickering dust that crossed the screen from left to right, unvarying in its speed and direction.' The mediated image, combined with the slow-paced description of Marshall's loss of consciousness, becomes a grim elegy for a society in its terminal phase.

For the construction mogul Hardoon there is no such thing as society. As the novel has unfolded, the reader has already been introduced, in brief present-tense interludes, to the erection of a huge structure using battalions of heavy earth-moving equipment behind giant windshields. The operation has been carried out with great difficulty and at enormous human cost. Kroll warns a protesting Marshall that Hardoon 'has just sealed out two hundred workers in Construction who'd been on the Tower right from the beginning.' Hardoon has some of the physical characteristics of a James Bond villain or even Dan Dare's nemesis the Mekon, with his 'massive domed forehead, small hard eyes and callous mouth.' Ballard borrowed the name from Silas Hardoon, a millionaire businessman and property developer active in Shanghai during the early twentieth century. Although Silas died in 1931, he had made his mark on the city, and his reputation as the wealthiest man in Asia survived into Ballard's boyhood. Indeed, Ballard, with his fondness for recycling names, had used Hardoon before, in an unpublished *Vermilion Sands* story 'The Hardoon Labyrinth', as Chris Beckett (2011) has pointed out. 'The real Hardoon that Ballard remembers from his childhood was "an Iraqi property tycoon who was told by a fortune-teller that if he ever stopped building he would die, and who then went on constructing elaborate pavilions all over Shanghai, many of them structures with no doors or interiors." In Ballard's draft story, Hardoon's jumbled faux buildings are—like the structures on the Hardoon Estate in the International Settlement of Shanghai—obsessional shells, not real buildings at all...'

The pyramid that Hardoon constructs to out-face the wind is exactly that—an obsessional shell that contains only one room, where he can stare into the eye of the storm, a tiny chamber behind thirty-foot concrete walls that will magically preserve him while humanity outside is destroyed. For Hardoon in the apparent security of his tower it is not a cosy catastrophe but one that validates him as a hero, a rebel against the hostility of the natural world. 'I alone have built upwards, have dared to challenge the wind, asserting Man's courage and his determination to conquer nature'. Connoisseurs of conspiracy theory (or occultism) might enjoy Hardoon as an Illuminatus figure, the Eye in the Triangle glaring out over vistas of devastation, the ultimate Masonic Master Builder, an atomic age Pharaoh at the apex of wealth and power.

The action sequences that lead Maitland, Lanyon and their party to finally encounter Hardoon unfold fairly predictably, as a consequence of Maitland (perhaps implausibly) forcing their transporter to divert to Hardoon Tower and the bunkers beneath it. They are, of course, captured by Kroll and his henchmen, allowing Hardoon to lecture them at length about his survivalist philosophy and the impregnability of his pyramid. He wants his stand against the forces of nature to serve as an example to others and expects Patricia Olsen to document it for posterity. In the meantime they will be captive

witnesses to his grand gesture, confined to the cramped bunkers under the supervision of Kroll and his security men. The situation foreshadows other encounters with dangerous eccentrics in Ballard's fiction—Strangman in *The Drowned World* or Lomax in *The Drought*.

The resolution is perhaps predictable. The bunkers flood and start collapsing, but Hardoon in his chamber is unmoved. There is—inevitably—some generic gun-play and roughhousing with Kroll. Yet the real action is generated by the force of the wind and Hardoon's obsession—his own idiosyncratic version of embracing catastrophe:

> The room was in darkness, the sole illumination streaming in from the observation window. Standing in front of it, his face only a foot from the glass, was Hardoon, the flickering field of light playing across his granitic features like the flames of some cosmic hell. So completely involved was he with the wind that Maitland hesitated before stepping forward, as much held back by the intangible power of Hardoon's presence as by the sounds of the hurricane battering at the window.

As the earth beneath the pyramid collapses, the wind catches the underside of the base and begins to destabilise the whole edifice. Perhaps a structural engineer could work out the feasibility of a 550 mph wind overturning a 25000 ton concrete block. Although hard-core SF writers from Jules Verne onwards have done the maths behind such speculations, I suspect that Ballard was more focussed on finishing the typescript quickly—at a rate of 6,000 words a day—before returning to clear his desk at *Chemistry and Industry*. But he suspends our disbelief more than adequately:

> Through the open aperture he looked out into the huge ravine below, like the hundred-yard-wide working of a six-lane underpass. Dust and exploding gravel obscured its sides. hurtling out throughout the narrowing venturi but he could

still see the great bulk of the pyramid towering overhead. The ravine led directly below it, but at least two thirds of its base still rested on solid earth, the overhanging portion revealing the L-piece of the communicating tunnel jutting below. The pyramid had tilted by ten degrees, snapping the tunnel in half like a straw.

The final act is the total collapse of the pyramid, coinciding with a sudden miraculous slowing in the airstream, which saves Patricia's life as a huge section of wall topples against the wind, instead of being driven by the current. The wind begins to drop, almost as suddenly as the rain resumes at the conclusion of *The Drought*. Ballard has been criticised for an apparently arbitrary ending, yet such is the nature of the disaster novel—the universe is indifferent to the vagaries of human character and motivation. Some might want to interpret the ending as the last judgement of an angry deity, appeased at last by the punishment of the rebellious Hardoon, but this reading goes against everything we know about Ballard's personal beliefs and intentions as a writer.

'Analysing the author's hidden motives is one of the quieter pleasures of reading—and writing—science fiction...the real significance of the cataclysmic story is obviously to be found

elsewhere. 'Storm-Wind' is no exception, and anyone wondering why I've chosen to destroy London quite so thoroughly should try living there for ten years.'

Ballard's postscript to the concluding instalment of 'Storm Wind' in *New Worlds* seems almost flippant, but it relates directly to the ambiguous motivations behind our interest in disaster narratives, either as writers or readers. They offer us a vicarious destruction, a purgative annihilation that is an inescapable part of creation—and thus create a premature elegy for us and all our works. In that sense, we are all at one with Hardoon, gazing into the time-storm.

References:

Brian Ash (editor), *The Visual Encyclopaedia of Science Fiction*, Pan Books, 1977

J.G. Ballard, 'Storm Wind', *New Worlds*, September and October 1961

J.G. Ballard, interview by James Goddard and David Pringle in *J.G. Ballard The First Twenty Years* Bran's Head Books, 1976

Chris Beckett, *The Progress of the Text: The Papers of J.G. Ballard* at the British Library, 2011 - http://www.bl.uk/eblj/2011articles/pdf/ebljarticle122011.pdf

Christopher Daly, *British science fiction and the Cold War, 1945-1969* - http://www.westminster.ac.uk/research/westminsterresearch

Paul Green, 'The Day the Earth Caught Fire' - http://www.culturecourt.com/Br.Paul/film/DayTheEarthCaughtFire.htm

Special thanks to David Pringle for suggestions and comments.

The Poetics of
"Studio 5, The Stars"

Ballard's attitude to poetry was always ambivalent.

As prose editor of Martin Bax's magazine *Ambit* in the 1960s he insisted that his priority was ' to get rid of the poetry' while in *Miracles of Life* he describes poetry readings—accurately in some cases—as 'a special form of social deprivation. In some dingy hall a sad little cult would listen to their cut-price shaman speaking in voices...' He maintained that Christopher Evans' computer generated poems published in *Ambit* were 'not only as good as the real thing. They were the real thing.'

Indeed as far back as 1952, Christopher Strachey at the University of Manchester had programmed a Ferranti Mark 1 computer to generate a 'love poem' using a preselected vocabulary and syntactical structure, producing such lines as 'My wistful love treasures your sympathy.' In 1959, Theo Lutz in Germany used a similar approach on an analogue computer, employing nouns from Kafka's *The Castle* to create gnomic utterances: 'Not every castle is old. Every day is old.' Given Ballard's voracious appetite for news about the latest developments in science and technology, it is highly likely that he was aware of projects like this and their potential for fictional extrapolation.

Yet Ballard's oeuvre, whether fiction, non-fiction or interview, includes favourable allusions to poets like John Donne, T.S Eliot, and especially Samuel Taylor Coleridge. Although Ballard showed little interest in literary manuscripts as fetish objects, he admitted that if he was given the original Ms of *The Rime of the Ancient Mariner* he would certainly 'look after it.' In an article 'Which Way to Inner Space?' published in *New Worlds* 118 in May 1962, after the appearance of 'Studio 5, The Stars' in January 1961, Ballard praises Ray Bradbury as 'a poet...(who)...can accept the current magazine conventions and transform even so hackneyed subject as Mars into an enthralling private world.'

Throughout his writing the terms 'poet', 'poetic' and 'poetry' recur in different contexts, often signifying a heightened state of awareness or surreality. 'The poetry of strange hotels' forms part of his credo in *What I Believe*, while he responds to the 'poetry' of Chris Marker's *La Jetee* or Jean Cocteau's *Orpheus*. In 'The Voices of Time', his superb elegy for a dying cosmos, beings from Orion communicate 'in poetry', although the astronauts who receive the communication can only translate it into 'poetic ramblings'. Elsewhere, writing poetry signifies an intensified, if fragile, mental state. In 'The Assassination Weapon' Coma 'spends all her time writing poems on the damaged typewriter'. Poetry is also equated with the expression of an ultimate authentic identity. As Sangster warns the narrator Pearson in *Kingdom Come,* 'Violence is the true poetry of governments'.

Stylistically, Ballard's writing, driven by dream-like imagery, extended metaphor and surreal similes, often operates as prose poetry in the manner of Baudelaire, Rimbaud, or Isidore Ducasse, author of the proto-surrealist text *Maldoror.* Although Ballard always stated that the visual artists of the Surrealist movement like Dali, Ernst, or Tanguy were far more potent sources of inspiration than surrealist poetry, there are perhaps echoes of texts like Andre Breton's *The Magnetic Fields* in the cadence of Ballard's long sentences and labyrinthine subordinate clauses.

Ballard's ambivalence to poetry as a genre may have been partially caused by the parochialism of the British poetry world in the 1950s and early 60s. In 1960, when Ballard wrote 'Studio 5, The Stars', prior to its appearance in *Science Fantasy* in January 1961, the UK's best selling poetry collection was John Betjeman's *Summoned by Bells*. This nostalgic blank-verse autobiography detailing Betjeman's cosy Edwardian childhood and his failure as a Divinity undergraduate at Oxford would doubtless had little appeal to the former inmate of Lunghua Camp.

Establishment poetry magazines like *The Poetry Review* and the *London Magazine* were dominated by Georgian pastoral poets like the followers of Edmund Blunden or disciples of the Movement, a British group centred around poets like Philip Larkin, John Wain and Kingsley Amis (later to briefly befriend Ballard) who wrote from an Anglocentric viewpoint in a realist mode, often self-deprecating and ironic, using traditional stanza forms and rhyme schemes. Of course, other voices were emerging, typified by Michael Horovitz's *New Departures* magazine, founded in 1959, which introduced poets from the European and American avant garde to a UK audience and promoted poetry as performance, often with jazz.

A key book was Donald M. Allen's 1960 Grove Press anthology

The New American Poetry featuring charismatic figures from the Beat scene, like Allen Ginsberg, Jack Kerouac, Gregory Corso and Lawrence Ferlinghetti, as well as pioneers in experimenting with form like Charles Olson. Although their work was to have a huge influence on the young British poets of the 60s like myself, they were frequently reviewed with hostility by the British literary establishment—a conflict which continues to this day, in different guises. However, Ballard showed no interest in Britain's poetry wars. After he had achieved professional status as a full time writer, supporting a young family as a single parent in the suburbs, he seems to have had little patience with poets who networked frantically at London launch parties and demanded repeated subsidies from the Arts Council for their 'amiable hobby', as he describes it in *Miracles of Life*. The psychologist Wilder Penrose in *Super Cannes* includes poets among 'those who aren't net contributors to society' along with 'traffic wardens and ecologists.'

'A coastal (sic) paradise where the "long hairs" idled their time away'. Ted Carnell's intro in *Science Fantasy*, back-referencing previous stories from the *Vermilion Sands* sequence, implies that this new piece might be a straightforward satire on the follies and excesses of a poetic sub-culture. But the work is complex and multi-levelled. As in other *Vermilion Sands* stories, the narration is first-person and reflective. The *mise-en-scene* of 'this over-lit desert resort... somewhere between Arizona and Ipanema Beach,' to quote from Ballard's own introduction to the 1985 Everyman edition, is quickly established. For Ballard it is 'a place where I would be happy to live.' Its crimson dunes dotted with post-modernist ultra-detached dwellings are a playground for exploring new technologies of hedonism and aesthetic experiment.

Apart from the electro-mechanical Verse Transcribers favoured by the poets of the colony, the only overtly 'science-fictional' elements which are typical of the magazine conventions of the period are the venomous sand-rays who might have flown out of Ray Bradbury's *Martian Chronicles* or even Edgar Rice Burroughs' Red Planet. The automated versifying provides a working premise for the fiction but

Ballard's preoccupations are, as always with landscape, mindscape and the psychic depths. The story becomes a magical fantasy playing subversively with myth and the archetype of the feminine as 'other'. Its polysemic imagery and wealth of symbolic references carry the resonance of an extended prose poem.

Initially the narrator Paul Ransom, poet and editor, is overwhelmed by a surfeit of poetry. Frail multi-coloured tapes 'with the texture of rose petal' drift across his verandah and into his living room. They emanate from Aurora Day, his reclusive neighbour at 'Studio 5, The Stars'. Those unsolicited contributions are imprinted with fragments of Shakespeare 'Sonnet 18' and Ezra Pound's 'Canto I', among other long dead bards.

Their fragmentation suggests the instability of his neighbour's mind but could also be read as an elegy for the erosion of the Western poetic canon over time. One is reminded of T.S. Eliot in *The Wasteland*: 'These fragments I have shored against my ruin.' The ribbons of text float like streams of ectoplasm from the body of a medium, contrasting with the tapes and punched cards of an IBM Verse Transcriber or a Philco Versomatic, the technology—now engagingly retro—that Ransom uses to edit *Wave IX*, an 'avant-garde poetry review'.

Surely Ballard is being ironic. For the submissions to *Wave IX*, which include 'a pastiche of Rupert Brooke' are anything but avant-garde or modernist. As editor, Ransom's primary duty is to tweak the contributions with the aid of his VT set, correcting the prosody, rhyme schemes and stanza forms in accordance with traditional notions of poetic craft. Poetry is represented here as an art-form in stasis, self-referential, pre-occupied with technique and mediated by a technology that requires only minimal human intervention.

Ransom's first response to his neighbour's unwelcome barrage of classic poetry is to send a polite note, like an affronted Shepperton suburbanite complaining of strange goings-on at 36 Old Charlton Road. It is ignored. When he tries to see her in person, the story veers towards myth, even the occult. For the sinister chauffeur/minder on the driveway resembles 'the God Pan...in a Cadillac,' with a club foot and 'a twisted face

WAVE IX

like a senile faun.' This Pan is not the benign deity of Kenneth Grahame's *Wind in the Willows* but the manic magical Pan 'all begetter, all destroyer', as hymned by Aleister Crowley, or William Burroughs' apocalyptic God of Panic, whose piping 'brings down the sky.'

The chauffeur takes a small flute from his pocket and starts to play 'some high irritating chords.' One could note in passing that 'chords' are virtually impossible to play on a monophonic wind instrument like the flute—a phrase that reveals Ballard's cheerful indifference to music. But what ensues is the first of several curious psychic attacks, of the kind described in Dion Fortune's *Psychic Self Defence* or accounts of alleged magical battles between squabbling members of the Hermetic Order of the Golden Dawn in the 1890s. The chauffeur's music evokes a micro tornado, a dust squall that envelopes Ransom and forces him to retreat, 'the dust flicking across the surface of the dunes on either side.'

One night Ransom sees Aurora from his balcony, a mysterious figure as enigmatic as one of Paul Delvaux's somnambulistic beauties. Radiating light from her gown, she progresses along the dunes accompanied by a retinue of hovering sand rays. She is 'lost in some deep reverie or dream' murmuring a sentence from Homer's *Iliad* that refers to the Judgement of Paris, implying perhaps that she craves validation of her beauty through the praises of her poets. Ransom saves her from wandering into the mouth of a sand reef and in return he is invited to cocktails the following day. Given Ballard's liking for cinema, one wonders if his portrayal of the Ransom/Aurora relationship was influenced by Federico Fellini's *La Dolce Vita*, which was released in 1960. In an interview for the German SF magazine *Quarber Merker* in 1976 he states 'this film made a great impression on me.' The central character Marcello, a novelist with a creative block reduced to writing gossip columns, is fascinated by the film star Sylvia, memorably played by Anita Eckberg, who is remote, mysterious, unpredictable, demanding the worship of the tabloid scribblers, while the 'beach fatigue' of the artistic demi-monde of the Sands trapped in their own version of 'the sweet life' resembles the ennui experienced by Fellini's high-society socialites.

Like the eponymous heroine of Andre Breton's poetic novella *Nadja*, Aurora at first seems totally dissociated, drifting from one level of consciousness to another even in mid-conversation, as if in a surrealistic trance. However, she is sufficiently focused to ask Ransom 'what is wrong with modern poetry?' He admits that the VT set has killed his own impulse to write. His stance here is typically Romantic, stressing the primacy of the poet's 'inspiration' and the importance of 'self-sacrifice' as a condition of 'mastering his medium.' The preferred reading of 'medium' in this context is 'language' but it is tempting to wonder if there is some unconscious slippage here, playing with connotations of an oracular 'medium' who must be 'mastered', a specifically masculine verb applied to a potentially female subject .

Aurora's own poems are, in Ransom's view, pseudo-oracular 'minatory and obscure like the oracular delirium of an insane witch', filled with rhetorical invocations and archaic diction that echoes Milton and Virgil. His fellow editor Tony Sapphire is equally dismissive, although he is surprised to learn that her pieces were composed without the aid of a computer. Like a typical tyro poet, she continues to bombard them with multiple submissions, either hand-delivered by her chauffeur or somehow embossed on the floating streamers. (Ransom notes that these are 'too fragile to have passed between the spools and high-speed cams of a computer mechanism', which invokes the image of some steam-punkish Babbage engine).

These, of course, are rejected. For many poets psychic assault on an editor is an understandable response to a series of rejection slips. Ransom begins to suffer from uneasy dreams and nearly has an unpleasant accident when he sits on a sand ray on his patio. After sending Aurora yet another terse rejection note, 'a colossal boil' develops on his cheek.

Fellow poet Raymond Mayo feels that Aurora embodies some dangerous primal force, 'formless and unstated.' She reminds him of 'Dali's Cosmogenic Venus' and makes him realise 'how terrifying all women really are.' In this context it's interesting to refer to Ballard's comments in a 1984 interview with Peter Ronnof-Jessen for *The Literary Review*. The interviewer suggests that his female characters are 'alluring but not very nice people.' Ballard responds at some length, pointing out that 'in fabulation women tend to be rather inscrutable' and 'their inscrutability is necessary for... the exploration voyage on which the hero is embarked.'

Then, having alluded to 'the lamia, the nightmare Life-in Death figure in Coleridge's *Ancient Mariner*' he adds that 'women tend to take up these rather threatening, sinister magical roles'. He then refers to Robert Graves' concept of the White Goddess, 'the not necessarily benevolent Muse'—It's hard not to see this archetypal concept of the Muse incarnated in Aurora whose 'slim, white-skinned face' has mesmerised Ransom.

Yet Ransom's refusal to accept Aurora's work is final, for the issue has gone to the printer. Then, when the copies are delivered, he is faced with a further demonstration of her power, for all his content has been somehow replaced by her work. She watches from her balcony as he burns the entire edition, triggering a full-scale magical offensive. Fragments of Keats, Ben Jonson, Shakespeare and other poets are rapidly inscribed on his door, his walls, his furniture and even tattooed on his own skin which becomes 'a living manuscript in which the ink still ran'. He now embodies the texts of the poetic canon he has betrayed. The terrifying phenomena cease only when he concedes defeat.

Aurora explains that the wellsprings of poetic inspiration are discovered through the enactment of myth—specifically the fable of Melander, Muse of Poetry and her lover Corydon. His companion poets have taken their gift for granted and lost their creative potency. Thus Corydon, whose devotion to Melander has sustained his creativity, sacrifices himself on behalf of his comrades to restore their gift. His story is displayed on a mural across the walls of Studio 5.

Ransom is unconvinced and decides to perpetrate a literary hoax against Aurora by programming his computers to produce a pastiche of neo-romantic verse. But his VT sets, like all the machines in Vermilion Sands, have been trashed beyond repair, vandalised, no doubt, during nocturnal visits from the chauffeur, the senile delinquent Pan. His only option for re-launching *Wave IX* is to persuade would-be contributors to write some self-penned material, a prospect that alarms them. As Tony Sapphire admits, 'Fifty years ago a few people wrote poetry, but no-one read it. Now nobody writes it either.' Sapphire's own opus—which he has not backed up—was 'ten million words long... a gigantic grotesque' while Ransom had been generating a 'transliteration of Joyce's *Ulysses* in a Greek setting', a reference perhaps to Ballard's abortive attempt to write a Joycean epic as a young man and a side-swipe at the obsolescent literary novel.

Ransom's final ploy is to persuade a virile young poet, Tristram Caldwell, to write some hand-made poems to fill the new edition. The lyrical style and classical themes of the resulting submission are 'thoroughly retrograde', but everything that Aurora might ask for. However, Ransom believes that Caldwell is still covertly using a VT set and the flaws in his metrics are caused by hardware problems like 'worn tapes on the rectifier circuit and a leaky condenser'. Nevertheless he badgers Caldwell for more, although the young poet complains he can only write one sonnet a day. Inevitably one is dedicated to Aurora...

Although Ransom is perversely attracted to Aurora he introduces Caldwell to her. But 'beach fatigue' dulls any resentment arising from their ensuing affair. He and Mayo join the couple on a sand-ray hunt through the galleries and ravines of the reefs at Lagoon West, approached via 'the old abstract film sets nearby', like the derelict sets and props around Shepperton studios, where Ballard's children played, as described in *The Kindness of Women*. The group soon splits, Caldwell accompanying Aurora while Ransom is joined by Mayo. The chauffeur collects the creatures that have been shot, 'his hunched figure hung about with the nets of writhing rays'.

The supposedly venomous sand-rays swoop and dive around them, prompting Mayo to fire his spear gun. There is a foreshadowing of the sacrificial theme, for Mayo is convinced that a ray he shot actually sang in its death throes, as if its expiry released a spectral music for the Muse, similar to the ancient Greek myth of the dying swan. Yet Ransom notices the chauffeur replacing 'something in his pocket', by implication the tiny but subversive Pan-pipe. Aurora also exploits the power of sound, a trope in several Ballard stories like 'The Sound Sweep' and 'Track 12', when she sings to the rays, ostensibly to entrap them, like a siren of the cavernous reefs. Her voice resonates through the cathedral-like chambers, provoking the angry and confused rays to lash out. Caldwell struggles to deflect them from Aurora. When she warns him that the escape route from the chamber is blocked, his frantic attempts to fight back invite a mass onslaught which apparently kills him.

As Aurora and the chauffeur hurry away towards the Cadillac, Ransom discovers that the supposedly 'blocked' escape via a crevice is actually clear. Aurora has deliberately created an ambush for her poet-lover, forcing him to sacrifice his life in the course of saving hers. Yet the whole episode has been a grotesque ritual, a bizarre work of performance art. When Ransom returns to his villa he finds Caldwell alive and well. Aurora has been deceived. Caldwell knew that the stings of the rays were non-lethal during the summer season but decided to act out the myth for Aurora's benefit. Thus the enactment of the narrative is artificial, like all art. To use a familiar quote from Jean Cocteau, who surely would have been a happy resident of Vermilion Sands 'art lies in order to tell the truth'—in this case to affirm the power of the female archetype.

Following the fabulated violence of Caldwell's pseudo-death, all twenty-three 'registered poets' in the Sands recover their creative power and produce stanzas dedicated to Aurora, the Muse-figure appeased by a simulated sacrifice. Even Ransom is impelled to write again, in touch once more with his subconscious. 'A dozen or so poems lay just below the surface of my mind.'

The story ends there. Ballard wisely makes no attempt to represent the reinvigorated talent of Ransom and his peers via direct quotation from their new work. With its preconceptions of the poetic process and its fabulation of an obsolete technology , one might read the story as an enjoyable period piece. But, like so much of Ballard's work it has acquired deeper resonance and relevance to some current cultural predicaments.

Firstly, it predicts the problem faced by poets in a post-modern digital world, i.e., the issue of readership. It has never been easier to self-publish on-line or with publish on demand, but never more difficult to attract readers or sell books in this new attention economy where there are so many new voices vying for your clicks and downloads. Across the English-speaking world there are hundreds of creative writing courses, producing poets who will doubtless go on to teach on new creative writing courses which will produce more poets who will...

In North America, and increasingly in the UK, a poet's career whether in the 'mainstream' or 'avant garde' (both unsatisfactory terms) is largely defined by his or her involvement in the academy and the recognition of academic peers. Today Ransom, Mayo, and their friends would be instructors on MFA courses, desperate to build up their bibliographies and meet productivity targets in the hope of become associate professors.

But 'Studio 5' addresses a more profound issue—the increasing ontological insecurity felt by practitioners in the creative arts as artificial intelligence becomes more sophisticated in emulating creativity. In 2015 Zachary Scholl, a student at Duke University, produced a computer generated poem, a surreal but coherent piece about environmental decay, which passed the Turing test, in that it was accepted unknowingly by the editors of the university's literary magazine. Ranjit Bhatnagar, another cyberpoet has designed Pentametron, which creates poems through harvesting and processing Twitter feeds.

Developments like this are unsettling for those of us who would like to believe in the unique quality of our human *qualia* and our ability to synthesise those insights in the quiddity of language. But I think Ballard and certainly his friend Christopher Evans would have been excited by these advances in digital creativity. Perhaps it is best to plunge into the vortices of the Singularity and take one's chances. As for myself, despite the lure of the Muse I shall search the thrift shops and surplus stores for a reconditioned Philco Versomatic in good working order.

References

• David Pringle. 'Ballard/Moorcock Chronology' *Deep Ends 2015*, Terminal Press, Toronto
• http://bonsall-books.co.uk/concordance/index.htm (J.G. Ballard— The Concordance by Mike Bonsall
• https://grandtextauto.soe.ucsc.edu/2005/08/01/ christopher-strachey-first-digital-artist/
• http://motherboard.vice.com/read/the-poem-that-passed-the-turing-test
• http://glia.ca/conu/digitalPoetics/ prehistoric-blog/2008/07/16/1959-theo-lutz-stochastic-text/

SHADOW
PEOPLE

The light on his helmet flickered across a heap of rubble at his feet. Some disturbance must have obstructed his exit while he was below—and for a few seconds Skelton feared that the cavity would collapse around him. Piece by piece he carefully moved the stony debris aside and twisted his body into the crooked shaft. Thankfully he could now see light in the cave mouth. Ignoring the bruising to his elbows and thighs, he squeezed his way up to the surface.

He'd been underground in the Barrowdale cave system for some hours, and now the setting sun was hidden by thick cloud. It was uncomfortably humid. He sat for a moment, breathing heavily before removing his helmet and surveying the empty landscape. Already the drifting overcast and the vista of empty moorland made his brief trauma in the cave more remote. He reminded himself that he'd known worse. And he wasn't going to stop caving, despite Helen's neurotic nagging.

He rummaged around inside his pack for bottled water. Then he extracted a cereal bar from a side pocket and chewed it slowly. The moor was silent, a heavy silence. No bird song or bleating sheep—strange for the North Lancashire dales.

Checking his old Rolex, he set off down the rough track that led back to the road. Helen would be having one of her panic attacks. With grim amusement he imagined her giving some absurd appeal at a police press conference: "Robert Skelton is lean, brown, weathered, cerebral but tough, 39 years old, shaven head, last seen wearing combat trousers and a dirty khaki jacket, digging himself into a hole..."

After twenty minutes he arrived at the Land Rover and pointed his key at the vehicle. Yet there was no flash of lights or click of locks. He tried again, cursing over-sophisticated gimmickry, tugging in vain at door handles. The central locking must have seized.

Skelton pulled out his mobile and selected "RAC Emergency Call Out"—to hear a burst of white noise followed by silence. Then he tried "Helen", only to hear more distortion and hiss—maybe with a hint of a voice in the mush? But the sound soon morphed into static, so he couldn't even leave a message. He was obviously too far from the nearest transceiver mast—more over-hyped technology. Frustrated, he pulled out the rock drill he'd used for placing anchors and began grinding with increasing ferocity at the rear hatch.

Eventually he succeeded in forcing the lock, which had never been fully secure since Helen backed the vehicle into a concrete pillar. He crawled into the back seat and peeled off his caving overalls. The car radio was dead, unsurprisingly, and after a brief burst of activity the sat-nav died as well. No joy with the ignition, as he feared. He prised open the hood, found a circuit tester in his tool kit and applied it to the battery terminals. The Land Rover's electrics seemed to be completely fried.

He opened his Ordinance Survey map and traced the route to Thornbury, his dormitory village. He was facing a long walk over the hills. But someone using the B-roads might give him a lift, even as night was falling. He would leave most of his gear in the marooned 4X4 and take his chances.

Tugging on a rucksack containing a few essentials, he set off, beside the dry stone walls bordering the single track road, and after an hour came to the fork with the signpost to Thornbury. It was getting dark. He looked for the glare of headlights but the road was deserted. Despite the humidity and an ache in his thighs he had to slog on.

About a quarter of a mile down the Thornbury road, he sighted a stationary car, awkwardly parked, almost in the centre of the road. It would be ironic if it had broken down through an electrical fault. He quickened his pace to offer assistance. Then, as he approached the rusty Vauxhall, he realised it was empty. The driver had obviously gone to seek help.

An odd luminous haze was gathering along the horizon. He sat and consulted his map, trying to work out where it emanated from—perhaps a temperature inversion of light pollution from Preston or Colne. Cushioned by his pack, resting against the stones of the low wall, he became aware of how tired he was. He was drifting...

A vast black sphere with an oily sheen hovered only a few hundred feet above the moorland. He understood

57

it was the latest version of the sun, the newly-grown black sun. But it was swelling horribly, bellying out to bud into great black polyps that obscured the starscape. Helen's face was projected across its complex curvatures, tiny and distorted. No sign of his daughter Becky. Helen's twisted lips worked furiously as she morphed into a news-reader, sternly announcing that there was no need for the public to go on panic-buying sprees. The droning industrial music behind her intensified to drown her admonitions...

He woke, cramped and sweaty, shaking out the dross dream. Another time-lapse. It would be dawn soon. He was still at least five miles from Thornbury but *en route* he would pass through Lordbridge, where he could buy food and drink, and hopefully task the local garage to send a pick-up truck for the Land Rover.

The sun was hidden behind a thickening grey membrane of cloud, but the heat was already becoming uncomfortable, as he trudged down Lordbridge's single deserted street. His mobile was still dead so he tried Helen again via the call-box beside The Seven Stars. No dialling tone, another failure of British Telecom's disintegrating infrastructure—although they'd probably try to blame it on solar storms, the currently silly-season story in the media, according to Helen, who kept up with these things. But the emptiness of the streets was disconcerting.

To his relief, the door of Lordbridge Service Station and Stores was wide-open although no lights were on. He strode across the forecourt, desperate for the bottled water and sandwiches he could see stacked on the shelves. The refrigeration seemed to be malfunctioning but he grabbed a couple of items and turned the corner of an aisle towards the counter—to find the proprietor sprawled on the floor.

Skelton knelt to check him out, but couldn't sense a heartbeat. The heavy limbs were stiffening, so the shopkeeper had been dead some hours. There were no marks of violence on the body, no signs of a break-in at the till. The gruff grey-haired man in his sixties who'd sold him petrol and newspapers had simply died on the job. Dazed by the increasing unreality of the situation, Skelton automatically put a handful of coins on the counter and wandered out.

Outside, his civic reflexes kicked in. He ought to inform one of the neighbours in the terrace opposite. But he felt an obscure reluctance to disturb whoever lived behind the drawn blinds. The police would know what to do. He'd contact the police station when he got to Thornbury, they'd find an undertaker.

He walked briskly out of Lordbridge. Moorland had given way to farmland, and maybe one of the farms on the outskirts would allow him a phone call. Then about half a mile out, opposite a big barn conversion, he saw a shape in the road, beside a mountain bike.

The rider was dead—a youth in an Iron Maiden t-shirt, maybe the paper boy on his way to work. The teenager's forehead was abraded by contact with the tarmac but once again Skelton couldn't find any other injuries. He hesitated for a moment before mounting the bicycle, but obviously his priority now was to reach Thornbury as quickly as possible.

As he cycled, he couldn't escape a flashback: Becky in her sun hat cycling around the garden on her pink bike with stabilisers. Despite the stabilisers she falls off. Helen is obsessed by the crackly kitchen radio so he rushes out to pick up his lovely squalling daughter. His calves strained and his heart pumped as he tackled the steep winding climb to Thornbury. By the time he'd reached The Moon Inn at the outskirts of the village, he had to pause for a moment and rest the bike against the beer-garden fence.

There must have been a ruck last night—only to be expected at one of Thornbury's rougher pubs. Tables, canopies and chairs had been overturned, broken glass covered the vomit-strewn paving. Cautiously he pushed open the door of the saloon bar. A beefy young man was slumped face down in a corner settle. Skelton felt for a pulse, flicked back the lid over a blank grey eye. Another corpse to report. His unease deepened.

Perhaps he should have shared Helen's obsessive fascination with media panics. He picked up a crumpled copy of *The Sun* from the floor. Headline: SUN SCARE? over a pic of the blazing orb and the predictable sub-head: BOFFINS DOOM SHOCKER!

He started to read but was interrupted in mid-sentence by a faint sound from beneath the floorboards, like a muffled cry. He padded warily over to the bar counter and peered over. A trap door led to the cellar. He had to go down, like it or not.

A young woman was curled up in the gloom among the kegs and bottles. A slight blonde in a disheveled halter-top. She seemed very disoriented, obviously hung-over.

"Please, Mister, pretty please. I'll come quietly. No problem..."

As Skelton helped her up, a semi-coherent back-story began to emerge. Apparently she was Emily, who worked weekends. She wasn't usually like this, she insisted. It was all the boss's fault...

"Big laugh, wasn't it—celebrating The End of the World— not that we believed it—just an excuse for an all night lock-in. A big fat piss-up. Cos I was well gone when the boss made me bring up some Budweisers. Must have fallen over and passed out. Wake up, Darren..." Emily staggered upright, crossed to the settle and started shaking the inert young man.

"I'm afraid he's dead, Emily. Like the others..."

She turned, open-mouthed, frozen. Then she lurched towards him, pummelling his shoulders with her small tattooed fists.

"What the fuck have you done to my Darren? Where's Terry, where's Kelly—what have you done to them?"

Skelton tried to control her outburst. Keep calm and carry on, the old Brit mantra. "I don't know what's been going on, I've only just got here. I'm sorry about your friend but—"

"You're a cop, aren't you? Trying to round people up for your stupid shelter? Well, you've been no fucking use here."

Until now, Skelton hadn't realised how seriously local authorities were taking this solar flare business. It must be at a very local level, for surely Helen with her constant monitoring of the national news would have told him, over and over, that there was a strategic plan for the whole country, and they ought to sign up for it right away, and he didn't care about his wife and daughter...

60

Another damned leakage from last night's dream:

he wants to have furious sex with Helen on the moors, under the slowly descending black sun, despite the steady rain of tiny insects. She's stretched out naked in a stone circle but she's looking over his shoulder, shouting at the sun as the sky darkens, and as he reaches for her, a black manta-like creature hovers over her, Becky at the edge of the circle clapping her hands at naughty mummy...

"Are you going to just stand there? Can't you get an ambulance or something?" Emily was sobbing now, kneeling over her boy friend's body, stroking his cheek.

Suddenly he had an urge—to help, to be protectively male. Clumsily, he put an arm round her waist and pulled her towards him, but she only screamed and wriggled out of his grasp.

"Dirty old bastard! Think you can come on to me, do you?" She snatched a pint mug from the floor and smashed it against the table. "I'll glass you if you try that again. Now just fuck off and leave me alone..."

He backed off, towards the door. No point in apologies. She was out of control, like Helen in one of her pre-menstrual arias. He should never have stopped. The emergency services would eventually catch up with her.

As he hurriedly mounted the bike, he noted a graffiti-style artwork on the cement rendering of the pub's side wall—a dark life-size silhouette of a man and a woman clutching each other. It looked very new. Helen would say it was cool, of course.

He pedalled down Thornbury High Town. The overcast was hotter and heavier than ever. Litter blew across the deserted street and the blank grey TV screens in the electrical shop offered no updates. An electric mobility scooter, maybe the one belonging to his awkward neighbour Mrs Garvey, lay overturned by the war memorial mini-roundabout.

He could continue straight ahead to his house on the far side of the village or take a left to the medical centre, where Helen would normally be seeing her first patients by now, having dropped Becky off at the nursery. He felt he should try the surgery first. Whatever this emergency was, Helen would be in crisis mode, almost relishing her role.

The surgery car park was empty—no sign of Helen's Renault, although she sometimes walked to work. But the graffiti artists had been busy again, depositing another murky humanoid silhouette on the whitewashed wall. The kids were out of control these days. They had zero respect, had to leave their marks everywhere.

The reception area was a shambles, as if the desk had suddenly been besieged by disaffected patients who'd torn out the phone, toppled the computer and scattered prescription forms across the carpet. Helen's office was unlocked and empty. He couldn't find her handbag so he guessed that she'd never come in. He checked the adjacent room used by Dr. Nosrul Ahmed, Helen's partner in the practice. No sign of his briefcase or umbrella. Odd, because the Pakistani was always punctilious and ultra-regular in his habits. Skelton was about to leave, when he sensed a slight movement in the curtains surrounding the couch in the corner.

He drew them back—to find a red-haired boy of about fourteen lying there, clutching his forehead, his face screwed up in pain. He tried to rise but was obviously disoriented, making random twitching movements like a damaged insect. His spatial recognition seemed scrambled, for he reached out past Skelton as if trying to open an invisible door in a non-existent wall.

Scrabbling in desk drawers Skelton found some codeine tablets and bottled water but the boy scowled and waved them away.

"Have you seen the other doctor, the woman doctor, Dr. Skelton? Where is everybody, what's happened?"

The boy gestured for pen and paper. In crude shaky capitals, like a five-year old rather than an adolescent, he wrote: SHADOW PEOPLE, mouthing the words silently, apparently terrified to speak. He began rocking back and forth on the couch, as if that might bring some relief from his agony.

Torn by conflicting guilts Skelton went out into the corridor. Treating the kid's mystery affliction would need more resources than a village practice could offer, probably an MRI scan at a city hospital. Shouting that he was going to look for more medication, he hid in a store-room for a few minutes and pondered his next move. There must be some emergency service that he could contact. But he needed Helen's car. It would be simplest to find Helen first.

When he emerged, he found Dr. Ahmed's consulting room empty. He rushed outside, to find that the bike had gone, too.

Exhausted from walking through the warm haze, he finally arrived at his house, the new-build semi that Helen had been so keen to turn into a home. The gate was still festooned with balloons and bunting for Becky's birthday party a few days earlier. There'd been another row about the timing of that, the clash with the University caving club outing. He'd done the right thing but passively resented it.

The door, unlocked, swung open. He called for Helen and Becky, half-hoping/half-fearing to hear Helen's bitter interrogation about his absence. But he could only hear a faint hum in his ears, like muted tinnitus. He riffled through opened bank statements on the hall table, looking for a note. She always left a bloody note. He paced from room to room. The house had lost power and the fridge in the kitchen had already started to smell. In the living room he knelt to finger the plastic bricks and birthday cards scattered across the rug among crushed crisps and chips, as if they could offer some clue to his daughter's whereabouts.

Helen's bedroom was empty. He groped through the dressing table and the bedside cabinet and flung open the wardrobe. The summer dresses, the smart trouser suits were all hanging there, like discarded skins.

His daughter's room—another blank space populated by surrogates, Peppa Pig and a fluffy swan and teddies. He peered under her bed—Becky loved playing hiding games. Suddenly conscious of his total exhaustion and nervous overload, he collapsed into her pillows. Wrapped in her Pokemon duvet, he sobbed himself into a broken sleep.

He was being squeezed through a hatchway in the riveted surface of the black sun. It was so hot in

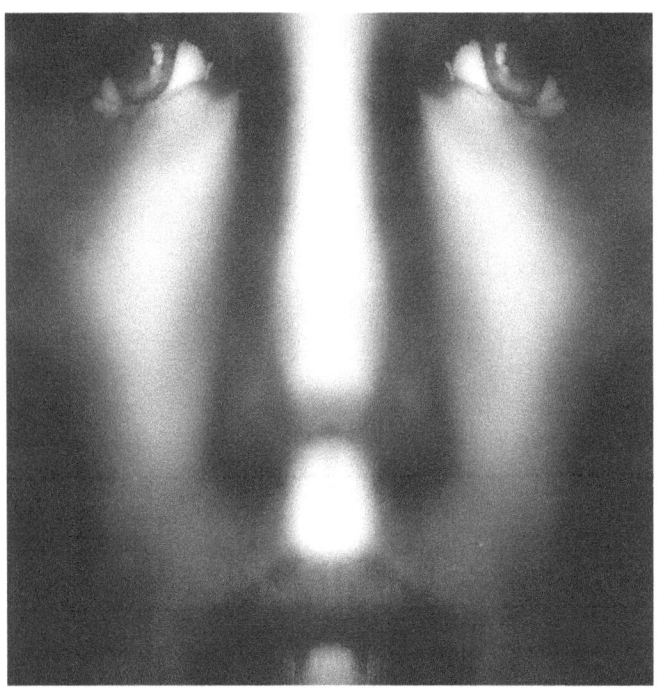

there you could hardly breathe. The burning rim of the hatch scarred his hands as he floated through thickening luminous fog. "Nothing's the Matter with Dark Matter," intoned Helen, resonating on some invisible PA, over distant screams. But Becky was being bottled into a time-capsule, one of the millions swirling through the time-smog which would eventually penetrate everything, everyone...

He must have slept for hours yet the ongoing nightmares had left him feeling drained and disoriented. In an attempt to pull himself together he washed and drank with cold water from the loo cistern, ransacked the kitchen cupboard for tinned food, and changed his clothes.

Another search in the master bedroom revealed Helen's diary, extricated from behind her bedside cabinet. He kneeled, flicking pages at random. *Rob edgy again/ So into himself. Won't even connect with B/ switched off the News right in the middle/shouting match/off to the bloody lab again—or one of his holes.* Then on an otherwise blank page: *DC—tonight?* with an exuberant floral doodle round it.

There had been another party three months ago. Helen had insisted they "networked", mingling people from her surgery with his colleagues at the University. All those smart professionals drinking and nibbling... They filled the living room with compulsive chatter over the thud of eighties rock. He'd escaped to the garden, watching the Chinese lanterns flickering in the evening breeze. Helen, usually so anxious to be at the hub of any social gathering, was sitting on the swing by the apple tree at the far end, in the shadows. She'd drunk more than usual. The bearded long-haired figure in jeans leaning over her and murmuring quietly was David Compton from the Physics Department. His students claimed he was "charismatic" but all Skelton could see was a fat hairy man smoking a joint and running long be-ringed fingers through his wife's hair. She'd laughed and turned her head away, before rising from the swing to teeter back down the garden path, Compton following her with a suave smile. In the kitchen, Helen had slipped past him, muttering that she was going to serve the quiche, while Compton immediately engaged Skelton in faux-jovial banter about their respective research targets and Compton's successful bid for Astrophysics funding (as opposed to the cuts in Skelton's Geology department).

The moment had passed but during it Skelton had seen a disturbing new erotic playfulness in Helen. He'd tried to suppress his awareness of it. But in the context of the diary, his fears of sexual dispossession might be real.

Skelton shouldered his pack and strode out of the house, on a mission now. He was half-aware that he might be talking aloud to the void but he no longer cared. He was going to have a good talk, give her a good seeing-to—and maybe smart bastard Compton needed to explain a few things. At least this was a conventional, even a banal reason—however painful—for her non-appearance. She must have taken Becky with her, too. Compton wasn't getting his cunning hands on Becky. Never trust a fucking hippie, he recalled. Especially slick ex-private-school fuckers like Compton.

Compton lived about two miles out, in a secluded cottage. Skelton was sweating, nauseous with rage, and desperate for a confrontation, any closure to his nightmare, but after a few minutes he had to pause for breath outside St. Andrew's, Thornbury's Anglican church, a squat grey fifteenth century edifice with a dwindling congregation in a nettle-infested churchyard. The sight of the crooked memorials with their eroded inscriptions triggered another flashback: Becky running off between the gravestones, playing "ghosts"/Helen calling her to come back...

He rested his head in his hands, shaking with misery. Then a gnarled hand touched his shoulder. A thin elderly man in a dog-collar stood over him.

"Have you lost loved ones? You must not despair, for many have been saved."

"My wife and daughter are missing..." Skelton couldn't articulate any more, it would be too painful to explain about her defection to Compton.

"I'm George, Reverend George Tupsley. I can take you to commune with those who are saved."

"I'm not a church-goer. I need to get on..."

"But they are truly saved. In the church. What is your name?"

"Skelton. Robert Skelton."

"Come with me, Robert. But you must be very quiet."

He felt a flicker of hope as Tupsley led him into the church. Candles illuminated rows of empty pews. Perhaps people were sheltering in the crypt—or behind the rood screen, which was draped with a huge golden banner, adorned with some kind of black and gold solar motif, obscuring the altar beyond. He began walking towards it, but Tupsley grabbed his elbow and gestured to him to sit. Skelton stared as the clergyman mounted his pulpit and began sermonising to the empty space.

"Some of our Christian brethren, quoting the holy prophet Isiah, have seen this mighty solar flare as a punishment from God for the sins of the irreligious. But if we consider Thessalonians 4:14-18, Corinthians 15:51-54, and Daniel 12:1-3 we can affirm that a great miracle has happened. There were signs and wonders in the sky. The Son of God became manifest as the Sun! Yet the angels have veiled His glory. The virtuous and the little children have been taken up in The Rapture, to partake of eternal life in Heaven! We are mere sinners, prone to the temptations of the flesh and intellectual pride and must stay on Earth to struggle in the Time of Tribulation. I beseech the Saved in heaven to pray for those of us left behind and bring us to eternal bliss—meanwhile God is punishing us with plague and sickness to purge our sins—until the Rapture comes again..."

Skelton rushed forward and dragged the Reverend out of his pulpit, wrestling him to the ground, almost strangling him in rage and frustration.

"Is this meant to be a joke? Don't give me your sick Nazarene crap. What really happened? Where's the damned shelter? Who are the Shadow People?"

Tupsley was on the edge of tears. "Please, Robert, I beg you... I know nothing about shelters—I was praying in the crypt. They are not Shadow People but People of the Light."

Skelton began walking away.

"Please stay with me, Robert. I'm starting to feel the sickness. The Unsaved will soon be pillaging our sanctuary. At least let us pray together..." Skelton left the Reverend praying to his new Solar deity in the flickering candlelight.

He found Compton asleep in bed, under a mound of dirty clothes and papers covered in scribbled equations. The blinds were drawn and the room was permeated with the sour odour of wine and vomit. He scanned the room, half-expecting to discover Helen's underwear or discarded contraceptives scattered on the expensive rug. It would easy to kill or maim Compton with a blow from the heavy ceramic bedside lamp; but the notion of attacking a sleeping naked man disturbed him—and it would take him no closer to Helen or Becky.

Instead, he shook him hard. Compton stirred, rolled over —and extracted a kitchen knife from the tangle of bedding. He lunged at Skelton, who stumbled backwards to the floor.

"Don't try anything melodramatic, Robert. Looks like I'm in fight mode and you're in flight. As usual..." Still feinting with the knife, he pulled on jeans and a t-shirt over his plump torso. "Now let's have a big boy's chat, shall we? You are owed some explanations, I suppose..."

"Where are Helen and Becky?" He'd intended the question as a fierce interrogation but somehow it emerged as a flat-voiced academic enquiry. He tried again, louder. "What have you done with my wife?"

"I've just done what any man would have done with a fragrant but neglected wife. Only three times if you really must know, while you were delving in the bowels of Mother Earth. It was cool. A consensual middle-class shag." He studied Skelton's thin twitching lips. "You really shouldn't act out the aggrieved husband. Not when you're on another planet most of the time. Anyway, none of it matters now, nothing matters, not a single damned thing!"

He hurled the knife past Skelton's ear, to send it thudding into the wooden frame of the bedroom mirror. Skelton tackled him by the calves and pulled him down, slamming his tormentor's head against the bedside cabinet.

"My bloody wife and kid matter to me, Compton. And you've abducted them, abused them—where are you hiding them, you arsehole?"

"I'm not hiding them, Robert. Honestly... it's been over a week since I last saw Helen, long before all this started."

Skelton remembered that afternoon when Helen had been especially keen to make a long trip to the nearest IKEA store, over forty miles away—but had insisted, unusually, that it was more important for him to go out and get on with his research. He'd never asked what she'd bought.

"Did you do it right here—in your squalor...?' He tried to get a firmer grip on Compton's windpipe. It would be good to feel him struggling for breath.

"Actually she wanted us to finish. Said the stress was too much. Maybe worried about fall-out on the kid—if you two split..."

Skelton's offensive faltered. "Not sure I believe you. I think you know where she is."

"You don't understand, Robert, you don't get the big picture.

They're probably—hidden now. In hiding, sort of. We just can't get to them. That's my working hypothesis..."

"Don't play language games, Compton."

"I'm playing a language game called science. Big science. You ought to respect that."

"You destroyed my family, you seduced the woman I loved..."

"Robert, we could be trapped in the most cataclysmic event in human history—do our petty personal melodramas really matter? You're a man of science in your way. Don't you want to work through a scientific analysis? It might offer some kind of resolution—even a way back for them...'

Skelton couldn't sustain his grasp on Compton, who picked himself up and grabbed a stick of bread and some cheese from a dirty plate on the floor. He tore the bread in half and offered a piece to Skelton.

"Go on, take it. And what's left of the wine." He indicated a half-empty bottle. "Could be in short supply very soon. Although I don't know about you but I've rather lost my appetite. Puking and the shits, all that..."

They ate slowly, in silence. Skelton had to struggle to control his gagging reflex. "Might as well go down to the study," said Compton, when they'd finished. "The laptop's blown, of course, but walled in by my journals we might have a temporary sense of security." So they descended the stairs, Skeleton taking care to tread behind the physicist in case he tried to fake an accident. He still half anticipated that Compton would open a closet and Helen's body would tumble out, wrapped in plastic garbage bags. He could only live from minute to minute now.

Compton rolled a joint and settled back in his office chair, as if conducting one of his famous seminars. "Well, let's consider the evidence. The flare's knocked out our electronics, far worse than we expected. Our guts tell us that we've probably taken a dose of gamma radiation. Now, have you seen the imprints, the body prints on walls?"

Skelton nodded. He had to try humouring Compton for a while. "But at Hiroshima, those were caused by a multi-kiloton blast of heat that took out most of the surrounding environment. These marks have been left on intact buildings, at random."

"Good point, Robert. Anything else?"

Skelton gave a terse account of the bodies he'd found, of his encounters with Emily in the pub, the boy at the surgery, the Reverend and his sermon. "The boy said there were 'Shadow People' while the vicar was babbling about his precious Rapture—usual fundamentalist rubbish..."

Compton shuffled the mass of scribbled diagrams and equations on his desk. "My theory might justify your vicar's sermonising. But with my computer down I can't develop it. We were, of course, expecting the flare to be the most powerful recorded—infinitely more powerful than the 1989 one that took out Quebec's power supply or the 1859 one that melted telegraph wires. Moreover, the ongoing coronal discharges have created an incredibly complex vortex of particles in the magnetosphere, a geomagnetic torus of accelerating quanta. You've seen the aurora pulsing in the night sky, even behind the cloud banks... Now the huge unprecedented discharges from the sun have coincided with complex planetary alignments, with Jupiter, Saturn and with the rim of the galaxy. For the first time in millennia this places Earth in alignment with the energy sources at the galactic core. I'm positing that these events have created a random space-time anomaly—a localised state of 'spasmodic quantum transition' that fractures the barrier between different world-lines in the multiverse."

"This sounds like acid-head physics to me. Surely everything would have imploded or disappeared? How can you explain the fact that there are survivors, even if we have been irradiated? Anyway I've never bought the Dyson-Deutsch multiple universe hypothesis... You bloody cosmologists need to get grounded." He eyed the door, plotting an exit from Compton and his fantasies. The physicist rose from his chair, blocking the doorway and gripped Skelton's wrist.

"Just hear me out. The anomaly—let's call it the Fracture —perhaps operates randomly, affecting tiny electrical currents in the brain. It's possibly set up abnormal resonance patterns in the Higgs-Boson condensate particles at sub-atomic levels of neural activity—including some kind of deep-level filter that protects us from *perceiving*—and therefore being morphed right into the adjacent parallel universes—your Shadow realms. The Disappeared have gone out of phase with us, if you like. The shadow markings on structures are just minor trace effects of the process of their transition, wherever...."

"You've smoked too many joints, Compton. This isn't getting us anywhere."

"In a few cases it might have been lethal. Hence the corpses. More people might have been genetically vulnerable to the effect—yet could cope with the transition states. And maybe younger people—children and adolescents particularly, always closer to fantasy realms, they'd be affected. Even a hard nut like you, Robert, must have had odd dreams and reveries in the last couple of days—leakages from alternate space-time..."

"More hippy bullshit..." It was unbearable. He would rather think of Helen and Becky dead and at peace than in some amorphous limbo-state.

"I can't absolutely prove it—but how else can you explain the relatively few bodies and the disappearance of most of the local population?"

"We've only been through a few small rural communities. If we went towards Preston I swear we'd find people there. There must have been a plan in place for setting up emergency centres. At the hospital or the university..."

"We won't be commuting by car, Robert. You're talking about hours of trekking on foot." Skelton felt gratified by Compton's unease. With his flab, the physicist would find it hard going.

"I thought you wanted to collect evidence..." But Skelton realised that whatever the evidence was, the conclusion would be terminal for Helen, and probably for him too.

The heat was overwhelming. Increasingly they were afflicted with vomiting and diarrhoea, squatting by the road to relieve themselves. In the car park of a Happy Eater they found two more bodies, a middle-aged couple slumped in the back seat of a BMW. Compton offered some new speculations about the effects of the flare but Skelton wasn't really listening. The only reality now was the rhythm of his boots on the asphalt. When they did agree to rest again, in a lay-by, Skelton found himself drifting into more invasive dreams:

Helen was waltzing with Reverend Tupsley in the aisles of the church, Compton leering at them from the pulpit, and Becky was painting it all into a big childish mural on the wall, which began crumbling away...

He awoke to hear Compton snoring and grunting. The dreams must be filtering through him as well. Once again Skelton realised he had the motive and the opportunity to kill his old adversary. A piece from a dry-stone wall would do it. Yet it would be meaningless, another addition to the statistics of non-existence.

Twenty minutes after they resumed the trek, Skelton checked his map. They should have been on the outskirts of Burnley by now. But they seemed to have retraced their steps, along the road that had led them past the Happy Eater. Skelton called to Compton a few yards behind but the scientist seemed absorbed in some purgatorial internal dialogue, a noiseless recitation of calculations. They turned a bend in the road, to encounter the signs for the diner where they'd discovered the bodies in the BMW.

"It's absurd," shouted Skelton. "We can't have taken a wrong turning." He checked the map again and looked at his compass.

"A waste of time," said Compton, catching up. He was displaying his sly smile now, as in the garden scenario with Helen. "It will just go round and round..." Skelton stared at the rotating needle.

"I suppose the disruptions in the Earth's geomagnetic field —".

Compton burst out laughing. "I think there's more to it than that. You'll see..." They walked on another hundred yards. "There's that vintage Jaguar," exclaimed Skelton, pointing to an abandoned vehicle, "there can't be two cars exactly like that in the area. We're definitely going round in a circle..."

"The rolling English road," Compton chuckled. "We might even be going round inside a sphere. Rocking and rolling our own ball of dung..."

"Stop it! Just shut the fuck up!" Compton's braying laugh was the worst thing about him.

"Poor old Earth-Man Skelton doesn't understand. I think the Fracture has created a space-time pocket, a cavity in the clumps of dark matter. It's as if we are inside a tiny bubble that has budded off from its root-reality. Our universe has effectively a radius of a few miles around. Thornbury is the New Jerusalem, the centre of the world."

"So what about the sky, the horizon? Fit them into your crazy world!"

"The World according to us is para-dimensional. It has no visible boundary because its topology curves in upon itself. We only have the illusion of a continuum." Skelton stared into the flickering haze obscuring the horizon. He felt stifled.

"Yes, it's a small world, Robert. You, me, Emily at the pub, that crazy vicar and the boy might be the only inhabitants." Compton was now laughing hysterically. Suddenly revitalised, he started running ahead, past the garden centre they'd approached over an hour ago. "First to find Emily fucks her. Or maybe we'll have a threesome. Then the vicar marries us all, to repopulate the world properly. Although with the radiation doses we've already taken, our offspring might not turn out too well. But no jealousy, Robert, you're in the Garden of Eden now!"

"There has to be a way out," yelled Skelton, "—something we can do..."

Compton stopped and gestured across the fields at the flickering luminous cloudscape. "This event's been triggered by the biggest energy discharge in the history of the solar system—do you really think we can cobble together some miracle gizmo to make everything all right again? The Fracture is a random fluctuation, like the solar flare itself. There's no way it could be exactly predicted, let alone manipulated. Given the desperate future we face in this contracted world it might make sense to kill ourselves ASAP. Or maybe we could have that final fight-to-the-death that you've been hankering for..."

He drew the kitchen blade from his belt, and threw it down in the middle of the road. "OK, as in the movies, the lethal weapon's up for grabs. Who's going to have the Darwinian advantage?"

Skelton sprinted but despite his weight, Compton reached the knife first.

"Let's fight for the territory. Winner inherits the earth." He suddenly jabbed the weapon at Skelton, who side-stepped him and began to run, veering off-road over the tussocky grass towards moorland, hoping that the terrain might slow his pursuer.

Skelton's wiry physique gave him the advantage for a while. And as he ran up the bumpy slopes the cloud cover descended around him to create a wall of clammy mist. Looking over his shoulder Skelton could only see a greyed-out shadowy outline of Compton, whose stream of breathless taunts and curses peaked and dipped as he struggled with the rough ground. Despite his stomach cramps and the rivulets of nausea coursing through him, Skelton forced himself to keep going. He at least was in touch with the raw earth, its turf, its strata of granite and basalt, its hot magnetic core. The unchanging gravitational pull that he was fighting with every ache of his leg muscles proved the fallacy of Compton's lunatic speculations. He would run his way out of this nightmare topography, just as he had forced his way out of the cave. Every step away from Compton was a step away from that fractal madness towards a single unified truth, however bleak.

But even this realisation couldn't sustain him indefinitely as a burning pain in his skull forced him to collapse at last on a mound of rubble. He shook off his pack, looking in vain for water and paracetamol tablets. Had he been running for minutes or hours? He'd lost his watch and any sense of duration.

He'd arrived at the boundary fence of a wrecked electrical sub-station on the edge of the moor. Through the barbed wire he could see half-molten transformers and deformed switchgear. A line of tilted pylons receded in the mist. And he could hear Compton closing in, still lecturing manically in the thickening gloom.

"...I know what you're thinking, Skelton, about the relationship between mass and gravity in a ball of rock. But that's in your old Newtonian frame of reference. The laws of physics are all mashed up here, giving you a reassuring virtualisation of gravity. I suppose you're planning to hide in one of your caves and play at being Neanderthals with Emily the barmaid. But we're going to have a different kind of ceremony..."

Skelton lay immobilised, as Compton loomed out of the mist, holding the knife before him like a dowsing rod. "You're wasting your limited space/time quotient if you think there's some way of restoring power. The sun-storm would have burnt out the transformer cores and fused the capacitors. But this is a good symbolic arena for our grand finale, mutually assured destruction amid the ruins of our technology..."

Sudden Skelton became aware they were being watched. A figure emerged from behind the low brick building at the side of the station. The pub girl Emily, grimy faced in her torn jeans, was waving furiously, apparently signalling for help. She must have walked for miles, thought Skelton—although Compton would claim his deformed local topology had mysteriously re-located her. Indeed, Compton had already switched his attention to her. "So that's our damsel in distress! What a pleasing materialisation! Let's do the right manly thing, shall we?" Skelton kicked his knee, pushed him over and for a moment they scuffled on the ground. Skelton grabbed the knife and hurled it as far as he could among nettles and coils of razor wire. He could at least deprive Compton of his theatrics. While the physicist was still struggling to rise, Skelton stumbled over to the doorway. A mountain bike was lying nearby.

Inside the station, beside the dead control panels, the red-haired boy from the surgery was curled in a foetal position on a pile of old newspapers. He was moaning, high-pitched keening noises that mingled with the mumbled prayers of the Reverend Tupsley, kneeling at the boy's side as he made ineffectual benedictions with a shaky hand.

"He's trying to tell us something. Can't you help him?" implored Emily. Skelton hushed the clergyman and bent over the boy trying to catch any phrases between the broken cries. He couldn't distinguish any words but with his aching skull only inches from the boy's brow he felt a terrible resonance...

...the black suns podded and burst across the starscapes; and now he was at the centre of the solar hole which was contracting around him, he was trapped in a sub-world in the galactic system of caves in dark matter and that was the hell that was the matter with him, just a shadow of his selves...

Compton was trying to tell him something. "Amazing! The boy seems have some pre-cognition of his personal Fracture. It's as if he was close to transition before but somehow the process was never completed. A Shadow Person on the cusp. You have to admit my theory was right..."

Skelton ignored him. Compton, Emily and the vicar were all irrelevant now; and there was nothing he could do for Helen and Becky. For the last time he tried to focus on them, in some defensive zone beyond the lethal glare of the cosmos. Helen clutching Becky's small hand on the rim of a dark pool/ Helen staring blankly as he ranted/Helen giggling nervously, unbuttoning her blouse for the first time...

Elbowing Tupsley and the girl aside, he dragged the screaming boy outside under the flickering strata of cloud. His brain throbbed as if his proximity to the boy only magnified whatever transition he was facing—but this was his only option now.

"OK, Compton, off you go to rule your little world. I'm staying here with the kid..."

"You're crazy, Robert. Much crazier than my physics..."

"So you're not to going to stay around, to witness empirical evidence, to see the Shadowing..."

Compton didn't reply as he retreated to the outbuilding. He would perhaps strangle Tupsley or rape Emily, but there was nothing more to be done in this current version of events. As Skelton gripped the boy's hand tighter, the landscape began solarising into a slow dazzle, its black/white pulsations

76

matching the rhythms of his neural pain. He touched the boy's forehead, attempting the desperate routines of consolation.

"It's OK, son. It's going to be all right. It's cool..."

Earth and sky dissolved into a white painless void.

When the policeman knocked at the door, Helen sent Becky up to her bedroom to play. In the living room the haggard unshaven officer put down his Glock and apologised for not having come earlier. He suggested she sat down.

"I'm afraid it's not looking good, Mrs Skelton. These were found on Penworthy Ridge, by the sub-station. We believe they belonged to your husband." From a plastic bag he produced an empty grey nylon back-pack and a broken Rolex.

Helen took the watch and turned it over. The initials 'RS' were just visible through encrustations of dirt.

"Yes—it's his all right. And the pack."

"I'm sorry, Mrs Skelton. We suspect that he must have met with a caving accident on the weekend of the flare. Unfortunately all our resources were very stretched—as they still are... I can't offer any false hopes at this late stage—and I don't know when we can get a specialist team into the cave system—to locate his body."

She tried to erase the imagery that was forming: Robert slowly asphyxiating in total darkness or struggling to regurgitate the rising water/his decaying body crammed into some subterranean cul-de-sac/his brusque dismissal of her worries that last nightmare weekend... But suddenly her bereavement was real, and she could feel tears starting.

"I realise it's a very hard time for you, Mrs Skelton."

She tried to rationalise things and regain control—Robert always said she was on the edge... "You say these were found on Penworthy Ridge. But that's miles from Barrowdale and his wretched caves."

"They could have been dropped by the same looters that torched the Landrover."

Helen shuddered as she recalled the anarchy that swept the country that terrible week after the National Grid went down, the rioting crowds that stormed the hospitals and trashed the stores, everything she'd dreaded and warned Robert about. Going with

Becky to her brother's remote farmhouse had been a wise move.

"I just wish I'd been able to call him. I did leave a message..."

"I'm really sorry for your loss, Mrs Skelton. There is a counselling service you can call once the phone lines are restored." He rose awkwardly from the sofa.

"Just one thing—Robert had a colleague—a sort of friend of ours, actually—David Compton...?"

"Another person on our missing list. It's surprising there are only a few, given the mayhem we've been dealing with. Obviously if we find anything else about your husband, we'll let you know, but—"

"So I ought to expect an inquest—accidental death—is that it?" It was time to show him out, get this whole thing over with.

"My sincere condolences, Doctor..." The officer turned and walked to his car, cradling the gun in his elbow. She sensed he felt relieved to have got through his script without too much overt melodrama. As she closed the door, she could hear Becky calling from upstairs. The child wanted to show her something, a drawing probably. TV was disrupted, it might not yet be safe to play in the garden—Helen didn't believe the official reassurances—so in her playroom Becky had immersed herself in realms of the imagination. Helen hurried up to inspect the offering.

Her daughter lay on her stomach scrawling slowly and deliberately with black crayon on a grey sheet of paper. At the top she'd drawn a number of black blobs radiating crooked spikes. At the bottom she'd outlined a kind of rudimentary hut and beside it a row of poles or masts.

"This is the bit the people want to show you," announced the child. On the wall of the house she drew a small crooked stick figure. Beside it she drew a larger erect stick figure. Then very carefully she drew a line to join their hands.

THE
FINAL
ANALYSIS

As his train crawled through the suburbs of south-west London, David Carlson was already having misgivings about his decision to have a consultation with Dr. Ballard. Perhaps he had been swayed too easily by his wife's insistence, repeated almost daily, that he was 'in need of psychiatric help'. He couldn't recall any specific incident that might have prompted Monica to make these assertions with such matriarchal solemnity.

Admittedly their conjugal relations had become infrequent and mechanical, as if they were clumsily acting out instructions from the advice column of one of the new 'liberated' women's magazines. He had also grown frustrated in his work as assistant editor of a trade magazine, *Plastics World*, a role that mostly involved re-writing press releases and enduring lunches with effusive company reps. And there were times when existence as a whole seemed to be a sequence of futile chores. Such feelings were apparently not uncommon in today's consumer society—he'd read that best-selling paperback *The Lonely Crowd*. But did he really need professional advice?

However, he was reassured by Dr James Ballard's CV. A medical degree at King's College, Cambridge, followed by training at the Tavistock Institute, a consultancy at the Maudsley Hospital and subsequent private practice at his home in Wimbledon. Even his substantial hourly rate seemed further endorsement of his status and competence.

Carlson turned his attention to the front page of the *Daily Telegraph*. PM ORDERS TROOPS TO VIETNAM. "Last night Prime Minister John Profumo told Parliament that soldiers from the Royal Marines and the Parachute Regiment would be flying to Vietnam to support US forces in their fight against the Communist guerrillas, now supported by Russian 'advisers'. An RAF squadron was also on stand-by in case of further escalation." Carlson was almost cheered by this news. At least Great Britain could still strut its stuff on the international stage. But he was discomfited by another front-page story RUSSIAN MOON LAUNCH RUMOUR? Control of the space ways, a recurrent theme in those Robert Heinlein stories he used to enjoy, would be a vital element in winning the Cold War.

Inside there was a frivolous item about the High Numbers

beat group. Their drummer Keith Moon had been arrested for crashing his Ferrari into an empty swimming pool, an alcohol fuelled prank that left him with a broken nose. Carlson didn't care much for pop music, although Monica still prized her Cliff Richard LPs. They were only in their thirties but this new twenty-something generation seemed almost alien as they paraded past their boutiques or flaunted their drug taking.

As the train drew into Wimbledon he began wondering what drugs Dr Ballard might prescribe.

After a brisk walk up Wimbledon Hill and a stroll through the upmarket Village, Carlson turned down a broad leafy avenue near the Common. He paused outside a large detached redbrick Edwardian villa with a half timbered facade. Through the shrubbery behind the clipped privet hedge, he could glimpse a blue Austin Cambridge saloon and a Triumph Bonneville motor cycle parked on the driveway. Somebody twitched a curtain. There was no way back now.

As he hesitated outside the porch, the door opened and a tall dark-haired woman appeared. "Do come in. I'm Marian Ballard. You must be Mr. Carlson. Jim's expecting you."

He was struck by her figure and her elegant accent as she ushered him inside, through a hallway cluttered with children's bicycles and scattered shopping bags. He nearly tripped over a small ginger cat that darted between his legs. "I'm sorry, Sputnik goes all over the place. He's quite bonkers..." She picked up the animal and cradled it in her arm as she opened the door of the front room. "Mr Carlson has landed," she announced cheerfully.

Carlson had been expecting some clinical antiseptic space, its geometry defined by functional office furniture and perhaps a few shelves of medical journals. He wasn't prepared for this dusty lair dominated by a battered mahogany desk and a faded crimson velvet chaise-longue. These were offset by rusty filing cabinets overflowing with folders, an old radio in a wooden cabinet, a large fan on a metal tripod and a tall potted palm by the window. A sagging bookshelf was piled up with tattered car manuals and recent copies of *New Cosmos,* a 'speculative fiction' magazine that he rarely bought now, wearying of its increasingly obscure fictions.

A tall man in his mid-thirties wearing a check sports jacket and dark shirt rose from behind the desk, and extended a hand. "Welcome, David... So you've survived your journey through the suburbs. Dangerous terrain. But interesting territory, especially when it becomes a journey into the interior. Or a voyage into the remote past. Imagine Jurassic Wimbledon, ruled by dinosaurs! Today, of course, our monsters roam the uplands of the cerebral cortex..."

Carlson could only mumble a reply about the train running on time. He'd been put off-guard by Dr. Ballard's affability and that rich drawling baritone voice. Surely a psychiatrist was supposed to have a minimal presence, a listener rather than an oracle? Meanwhile Ballard gestured towards the couch, so Carlson reclined on it, according to protocol.

While his doctor was sorting through paperwork and rummaging for a notebook, Carlson surveyed the room. A reproduction of Salvador Dali's *The Metamorphoses of Narcissus* was pinned to the wall beside him while a framed oil painting hung behind the desk. In the style of Rene Magritte it depicted a winged naked woman flying above a forest of umbrellas. He noted the signature—JGB. Unfortunately the composition seemed awkward and the brushwork looked clumsy so he felt might be wise to refrain from comment.

A model aircraft was suspended on a wire above the couch. From his viewing of war films he recognised it as a Mitsubishi Zero fighter, as flown by Japanese *kamikaze* pilots. He had a sudden vision of it screaming down towards his head as he tried to articulate his malaise.

'So where do we want to start?' Dr Ballard's jovial prompting aroused him from this morbid fantasy.

Carlson began with what he called 'an overview' of his situation, a long rambling narration regarding his unrewarding job and 'marital difficulties'. But increasingly he felt he was outlining the case history of an anonymous alien subject. His account of Monica's dutiful attempts to arouse him seemed like a heavily censored chapter from a mediocre erotic novel or a quote from a tabloid sex crime report. "The accused then attempted intimacy." The words went dead as soon as he uttered them. In the silence he could hear the tick of his psychiatrist's alarm clock.

Perhaps his narrative needed a context. So he explained how he was an only child who'd grown up in South London. His father was a minor civil servant, his mother a maths teacher. They were devout Methodists, protective, wary of change and 'influences'. Even skiffle music on the BBC *Light Programme* was regarded with suspicion and his selection of art books from the local library was carefully scrutinised. However, he'd done well at grammar school, in a low-key fashion, and gone up to Oxford where he'd begun a BA in English Literature. Unfortunately he failed the first year exams and dropped out. His family overruled his desire to attend art school and pressured him to seek employment. So began a series of dead-end jobs—waiter, barman, encyclopaedia salesman, all ending prematurely while he lived at home with his impatient purse-lipped parents. Then through a family friend he got an office-boy post with *Plastics World* where he'd been for over a decade, rising by default to his current position. He'd met Monica at an office party when she was temping for another magazine in the building. After their marriage they had managed to buy a flat in Surbiton although Monica now had ambitions for a three bedroom semi.

He couldn't keep this up. "It's no good. It's so drab, meaningless, one botched job after another, a history of failures. My wife keeps implying there's something wrong with me. And the worst thing is that I don't bloody care. It doesn't seem real, any of it."

The psychiatrist put down his pen. "How much television do you watch?"

"The news, both BBC and ITV. Monica likes to watch *Play for Today* sometimes but I'm not really a drama person."

"The news is a superior fabulation, I agree. But do you fantasise about intercourse with some female TV presenter—Joan Bakewell perhaps? In an abandoned studio, during a hurricane, for example? Or perhaps an actress—Jayne Mansfield in a Buick Riviera?"

"I really don't see the relevance..." Carlson was irritated by Ballard's flippancy.

"You must go deeper into your obsessions. Do you dream?"

"I don't remember any dreams..."

"That's quite unusual. A friend of mine, Dr Christopher Evans, is conducting some research on dreaming at the National Physical Laboratory. Chris hypothesises that we all need to dream, just as a computer needs down-time to reorganise its data. You'd be an interesting subject."

"I'm not a laboratory animal, Dr Ballard." Carlson resented the suggestion that he was a passive specimen, to be wired up and interrogated by men in white coats.

"Our animal inheritance goes back into the depths of archeopsychic time. Your brain carries the imprint of your reptilian and mammalian forebears, their memories of fight and flight across the forests and deserts of a very dangerous planet. In dreaming you can access their accumulated ancestral wisdom. You should start keeping a log and bring it to our next session."

The alarm rang and Dr Ballard closed his notebook. Carlson still lay on the couch, pondering this disturbing request. Then he felt Ballard's hand on his elbow, raising him from his supine position and steering him towards the door.

When he arrived home, he found Monica busy in the kitchen. She was wearing a red leather mini-skirt and she'd combed her blonde hair into a pony tail, like some French film actress.

"Would you like some red wine with your *beef bourguignon*, darling? After we've eaten you must tell me all about it. Then we can have an early night..."

They sat down at Monica's new G-Plan table. Carlson savoured the rich meat with a sudden primal satisfaction, as if he'd slaughtered the beast himself. He listened to Monica's animated dramatisation of her triumph over Mr. Stanwell, her rival in the Accounts Department. Thanks to her cunning wiles she now had priority access to the new IBM payroll computer. Carlson became quite absorbed in this strange soap opera. He could imagine a close-up of Monica's defiant pout, followed by a pan across the office to the balding Stanwell biting his moustache in high indignation. Then her scenario segued into an interrogation.

"So what did you tell Dr. Ballard? About your—"

"Not very much."

"But sweetheart—that's why we're paying him, isn't it?" Her coy smile couldn't conceal her impatience.

"I hardly got a word in. He was too busy playing the Sage of the Suburbs." Monica frowned, uncertain of how to respond.

Pushing his plate aside, Carlson got up and turned on the TV. The normally unflappable BBC news reader looked flustered.

"...claims that two RAF Hawker Hunter jets have been shot down over Hanoi have not been confirmed by the Ministry of Defence. Meanwhile Russian MIG-15 fighters have been observed giving air support to Viet Cong units making sorties into the Mekong Delta..."

Carlson switched to the commercial channel, cutting into an advert for skin lotion. A dark-haired girl in a bikini was emerging from the sea in slow motion, watched closely by a group of young men sprawled on the sandy beach. A female voice whispered over flutes and vibes. *With Solarise All Their Eyes Are On You.* Carlson was fascinated by the play of sunlight on her cheekbones and the smooth curvature of her belly and thighs, a calculus of desire...

His reverie was disrupted by Monica calling from the kitchen, demanding his assistance with the washing-up, but her words sounded as distant and cryptic as the cries of seabirds circling over that streaky monochrome beach. He turned the TV volume down.

Later he fell asleep on the couch.

SUBJECT: David Graham Carlson—DOB: 5th March 1933
Session 2: 17th August 1966

Today DC produced his dream log, carefully written in an exercise book like a piece of Latin homework. There are only three items in this oneiric record. Two of them are too fragmented and diffuse for close analysis, although they both have some interesting elements. DC dreamed that he was trapped by tangled seaweed in an expanse of warm brackish water that rose up to his neck as he fought off the claws and mandibles of a crab-like creature. He was afraid of drowning and woke up abruptly.

I recognised at once that this almost certainly referred to his marital 'stagnation' and his fear of breaking the incest taboo with Monica C as his mother-figure. However I believe that subject is not yet ready for this revelation so I suggested the dream might be a trauma narrative of uterine misadventure, perhaps entrapment in the umbilical cord, an interpretation that he accepted, albeit reluctantly.

A second dream, three nights later, seemed to centre on a motor accident. He was driving a large American convertible. A female mannequin in a blonde wig and miniskirt was seated beside him—clearly another reference to Monica C. Very loud beat music was playing on the car radio. This distracted him and he drove into the concrete pillar of a multi-storey car park. In shock he embraced the rubbery plastic limbs of the doll, only to find a policeman looming over him arresting him for gross indecency.

Obviously repressed desire and guilt are the key factors dominating his sex 'drive' although curiously DC has never owned a car or even taken out a provisional licence. The American car is another anomaly. Chris would say that it's been implanted by TV footage of that failed assassination attempt on President Nixon in Los Angeles.

The third account is the most detailed and coherent. DC is flying over Wimbledon Common in an ancient bi-plane. He is almost naked except for his helmet and goggles for it is extremely hot and a giant sun, almost twice normal size, glares down from an azure sky. The engine keeps cutting out and he is losing height.

He skims the tops of oaks and beeches, their foliage browned, their clusters of scorched branches and twigs resembling tangles of dead neutrons and synapses. Wild fires are breaking out in these woodlands so he steers through drifting pillars of smoke towards the golf course, which is now a wide expanse of baked cracked earth. He manages a bumpy landing, the aircraft collapsing around him and disintegrating into a heap of sand and rust.

He staggers away, desperate to find water and sets off towards the properties bordering the Common. Glancing back he sees a glistening metallic lizard of some kind tracking him slowly but purposefully. It's hard to move fast over the glassy outcrops of fused sand. But he succeeds at last in crossing the fractured tarmac of the road towards the luxury Parkside Apartments.

He pushes open the heavy doors—to find himself behind a giant movie set. The flats are literally flat, like the hoardings for some vast advertisement. Beyond as far as the eye can see there are sand-dunes, their blankness only relieved by the occasional protrusion of a television aerial or corroded girder. A few feet away a woman resembling Catherine Deneuve sits on a beach chair in front of a huge electric typewriter on a mahogany desk. "You are the last poet," she announces solemnly. As he wakes he knows this will be on the TV morning news.

DC has studied literature so I suspect there has been some embellishment and imposition of narrative structure. However what concerns me is the apocalyptic quality of this dream. It clearly presages some crisis, perhaps a psychotic episode that will break through his loss of affect and drastically change his relationship with his wife—for better or worse. I must bring forward the date for his next appointment.

MAKE LOVE, NOT WAR! TROOPS OUT! NO NUKES FOR UK! Carlson was deafened by the overlapping chants of the protesters, brandishing their placards like a forest of pitchforks as he tried to make his way around the edge of Trafalgar Square. The demonstration was apparently unauthorised, a spontaneous happening promoted by extremist groups like the Crypto-Anarchist Front and the Freakniks. Indeed, Freaknik girls danced naked in the fountains, splashing and screaming, hysterical Cassandras prophesying doom while a hairy poet perching on a stone lion declaimed through a megaphone. Meanwhile bewildered policemen were struggling to control the marchers as they swirled around Nelson's Column like pilgrims around the Black Stone of Mecca. The groups with black flags were clearly intent on breaking through to Whitehall. The crush could easily turn into a stampede.

Carlson desperately needed to get to Waterloo Station if he was to make this new and highly inconvenient session with Dr Ballard. He was already in bad odour with Burton, his boss, for leaving their Soho office early, having done a hasty sub-edit on 'High-Density Polythene—The Future of Food Packaging!'. But these scruffy boys and girls with their banners formed an impenetrable scrum across the pavements, blocking him in every direction. A bearded youth in jeans cast a hostile eye over Carlson's grey suit and tie. "Hey, it's a pig in plain clothes, trying to suss us out!"

Carlson ignored the jibe and tried to elbow his way forward but the boy continued ranting in his face. "You're a dead man, you know that? Dead to the world and you want us dead like you. Sorry for your wife, it must be like fucking a radioactive corpse." Two girls bedecked with flowers and beads burst out laughing.

Carlson, suddenly in fight mode, jabbed an index finger in his tormentor's eye. The boy lost his balance and fell, cracking his head on the kerb. To his own amazement, Carlson found himself stamping on the boy's skull again and again, as if he was crushing some venomous insect. Each adrenalin-fuelled kick confirmed his territorial rights. Blood trickled from his victim's nose and ears. The girls were screaming now, retreating in terror as he pushed them aside and ran towards Villiers Street and the Hungerford Bridge. As he immersed himself in the crowd he could hear the desperate cries of the young people as they attempted to revive their peace warrior.

"You have to help me, Dr Ballard. I may have killed somebody..." Carlson plunged into a garbled account of his encounter. The psychiatrist put aside his notebook and listened intently while Carlson reprised the narrative yet again.

"I felt everyone on the station concourse knew about it already. They all had their heads down hiding behind their evening papers, like they were reading the story, my story. They were dumb—except a few women crying. And the train was so crowded, even for the rush hour. Men, women and children. They told the children not to cry. It was like..."

"...like when you were evacuated during the war?" Ballard suggested.

Carlson remembered the farm in Newton Abbot, the surly family that reluctantly took him in. "Yes—how did you know? Were you?"

"In a manner of speaking. I was in the Far East. In a civilian prison camp. But enough of that. I sensed that you were approaching a catharsis. It's a pity you didn't come and see me earlier, when your psychosis might have taken on a more benevolent form, seeking release in the gentler interzones of fetishism, in the generosity of women."

"But what I should do now? There were scores of police there. And hundreds of witnesses. They must have seen me, even in that riot."

"I think the authorities have other preoccupations at the moment. You really need a drink. Would you like a scotch?"

"Surely that's not really ethical..."

"Oh, it's an essential prescription, especially in the current situation." Ballard poured two doubles and topped them up with a squirt of soda. He handed a glass to Carlson. "You see, this could be my final analysis. I've sent Marian and the children to North Wales, for the time being. I'm planning to join them tomorrow."

"I don't understand."

Ballard switched on the radio. "... interrupt this programme for a special News Bulletin. Following last night's incursion into East Berlin by a US task force, the Kremlin has ordered the British Ambassador, Sir Alec Douglas Home, to return to London, effectively breaking off diplomatic relations with the UK. In other developments, Russian and Chinese bombers have carried out heavy raids on Saigon and Viet Cong forces are now at the outskirts of the city. At nine o'clock tonight Her Majesty the Queen will give a TV and radio address to the nation. Meanwhile, citizens are advised to read the Civil Defence leaflets now being distributed..."

Taking a deep swig from his glass, Ballard turned off the set. "I think we're having a wake in advance for the megadeaths. Our

89

private Hiroshimas have become public Nagasakis. If I were you, Carlson, I'd set off now and try to salvage something with Monica. I've enjoyed having you as a patient. Your dreamscapes could have made fascinating stories."

"You write? From our case histories?" Carlson should have been shocked. But it seemed the inevitable thing to do, almost comic in the circumstances.

"I won a short story competition at Cambridge, that's all. Perhaps I should have stuck with it. But the literary life isn't for me. Nevertheless—." The drone of aircraft overhead obscured the rest of the sentence.

Ballard sat down at the desk, poured himself another whiskey and inserted a sheet of paper into his typewriter. Carlson hovered by the door, waves of emotion now rolling through his mind. He was paralysed by fear, smitten by an abrupt surge of desire for Monica, terrified of the void ahead.

"Go, Carlson—just go!"

He ran out into the dusk. All along Marryat Road householders were strapping suitcases to roof racks or cajoling their children into Volvos. There was already a jam at the junction with Parkside. Pacing himself for the long walk ahead, he was passing the War Memorial at the edge of the Common when he heard the first sirens.

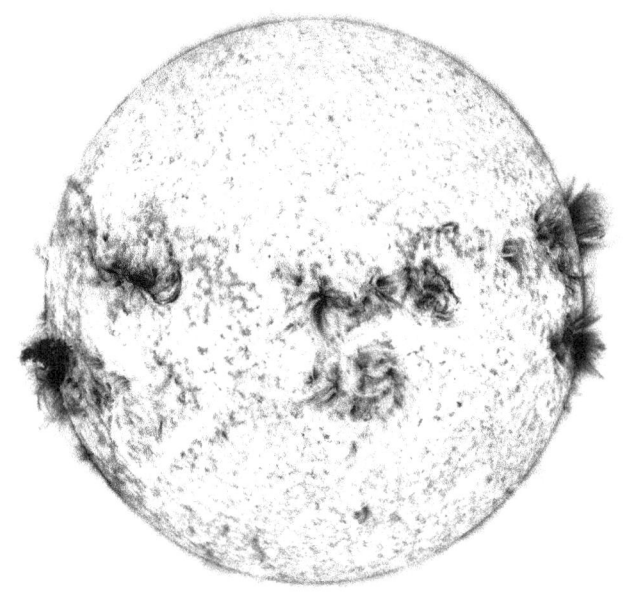

SUN POWER

Through a haze of smoke from the smouldering shrubbery at the edge of the Common, Helston caught sight of the Sun Temple. It was larger than he expected, as tall as the parched beech trees he'd hurried past before abandoning his Nissan hatchback, battery depleted, at the edge of this once leafy suburban parkland. The crude cone of baked earth and stony rubble spiralled erratically upwards, solar panels lashed crudely to its sides. A burnished coppery sphere was poised precariously at its apex. As if giant termites had built a helter-skelter—Helston struggled to erase the grotesque image, another symptom of his increasing disorientation since entering this new Panic Zone. He had no option but to skirt the muddy bowl of Rushmere Pond and cross a hundred metres of baked earth.

He was almost overwhelmed by the heat, 39 C according to his wrist monitor, an overload for a man in his sixties. Flies were busy at the edge of the pond, clustering over a dead Rottweiler, some urban warrior's lost war-dog.

Then he became aware of another movement, in the bushes to the right of the structure. A ragged boy of about ten emerged, dragging a skinny white goat on a chain. His narrow brown face was half concealed by a baseball cap and green goggles. Helston quickened his pace and shouted but the boy ignored him and continued an erratic path around the far side of the Temple, before veering off again into the bushes, past the rusting chassis of an upturned quad bike.

Helston decided to save his energies. He advanced over the cracked earth around the base of the structure, still keeping a couple of metres between himself and that dark lumpish wall resembling a carapace of some huge alien arthropod. It might leak globules of a lethal toxin, a malignant sun-sweat. He groped for the water bottle in his pack. Maybe a newly-imported virus was infiltrating his system. But he had to take control, stop this involuntary retching.

Then he saw the Temple Portal. Black windowless metal doors, industrial salvage perhaps, had been bodged into the stonework. And he could hear chanting voices—the deep drone of the Sun Priests.

"Adam Helston is an unreliable narrator," insisted Samira Qureshi. "We can't trust anything he reports back, he'll impose his own fantasies on the Zone."

"Are you sure he's not going to impose his overheated fantasies on you?" Fawcett enjoyed needling his elegant young colleague and watching her pursed lips. She adjusted her hijab and opened a new tab on her screen.

"Keep the male gaze to yourself, Karl. No time for frivolity —or manly exhibitionism." She glanced disdainfully at his bare chest and cut-off combat trousers.

He turned to his own monitor. She was right of course. Even down here in the Solnet London control bunker the aircon could barely cope. CCTV cameras across the city were starting to fail in the heat—Helston's official justification for his reconnoitre into the South West Sector. Panic Zones, arenas of excess and chaos, were spreading through all the twenty-first century conurbations as the temperature rose.

"'This should have been a peak for wattage.'" Samira scanned a flashing display of megawatt output from Solnet's various UK receptor sites. Over half were blacked out while the remainder fluctuated erratically. Was there a new problem with Cyclops, on geo-stationary orbit over the UK? Solnet Global HQ in Seoul was incommunicado again. But the issues might be closer to home, on the ground.

Fawcett remained silent, recalling the marketing videos of his youth. SOLNET, the international high-orbit Solar Power Satellite Network, beaming millions of watts down to receivers across the planet. Free Energy for a Freer World! As Earth's population bubbled up to the ten billion mark and Peak Oil dwindled to a dribble, desperate governments craved cheap energy. For a few years the grids of solar panelling that covered the North African deserts for thousands of square kilometres seemed sufficient to meet the consumer needs of the West. But 'rogue regimes' like the People's Republic of the Sahara began cutting off the power supply, to pressure Europe for its dwindling aid resources. The republics themselves were collapsing through drought and famine, so their solar energy infrastructure quickly became degraded by neglect and civil war. Bungled Western interventions triggered further surges of desperate refugees towards the Mediterranean. Samira's parents were probably part of the last wave to get through before Britain's beaches were mined and electrified.

"Stop staring at me..." Samira swung round on her chair and glared at him. "Focus, Karl, focus! Are we going to recall Helston from this insane expedition of his? We need everybody on board to service the receivers that are still working."

"Adam's intuitions have worked before. He warned Control years ago that those microwave rectenna farms across Germany were not going to be viable on the long run, that the UK was better served by a network of laser satellites like Cyclops."

"And now he intuits there's some great mystic out there that can solve a global crisis?"

"He believes Doctor Raymond may have some insights that could help us..." Fawcett knew he didn't sound convinced. Samira was already ignoring him, switching her attention to the latest video streamed from Wembley where clashing mobs had torched the stadium and were trashing local shops. The riots were getting closer.

Helston knocked for minutes on the Temple doors, at first with his fist, then with a stone. He could hear steady chanting inside and tried pressing his ear against the hot metal in a futile attempt to pick out the actual words of this solar litany.

Someone was tugging his sleeve. The boy with the goat had returned and was scrutinising him as if he was some tourist from Alaska who might be an easy mark for an edgy guided tour into a typical British Panic Zone.

"No good. I help you go in. But first water, innit..." The voice was hoarse but emphatic.

Even as Helston was considering this implausible offer, the child snatched the flask from his back pack and began guzzling its lukewarm fluid. When Helston grabbed it back, it was already half-empty.

"More!" The boy whined, tugging at the restless goat, his rank-smelling familiar. "You dry old man not need it. You only..." Helston's hand dropped to the taser on his belt and the boy fell silent.

"You can't help me. Go away."

The boy shrugged. He picked up a fragment of masonry and began tapping a quick intricate rhythm on the door. After a few seconds the voices inside peaked briefly before dying away. Then a door creaked open. Through his tinted lenses Helston found it hard to adjust to the darkness.

A dark-skinned woman in metallic robes was pointing a steel wand at him. Except that it was not a wand but the barrel of some improvised flame-thrower device, to judge from the hoses and cylinders strapped across her back—and the tiny pilot flame issuing from the nozzle.

"Go. Go now!" She jabbed the weapon towards Helston, then swivelled it towards the boy. "Why you bring this waste-man?"

The boy seemed unfazed. "I caught your meat, innit?" He pointed to the animal, tottering with exhaustion in the heat. The woman checked its scrawny limbs and protruding bones, still keeping the fiery tip of her weapon aligned with Helston's body. She shook her head. The boy removed his goggles and cap and offered them to her. "OK, you get extra tax. For Father Ray."

Despite the stifling air and stench, Helston felt a spasm of excitement. His intuition about Dr Raymond disappearing into the Panic Zones to re-invent himself as a cult leader was surely validated. But the woman was still weighing up the deal. She and the boy were bartering now in a rapid patois he couldn't follow.

Finally they seemed to reach an agreement. And he was apparently part of it, as a masked man stepped out of the shadows to drag the goat inside, while the woman gestured for him to follow. The tiny flame from the long barrel flickered inches from his jaw. "You own the waste-man, own the old waste-man," screeched the boy as he scampered off into the heat haze, Helston's backpack on his shoulders. Helston staggered through the darkness across the irregular masonry of the Temple floor. Somebody was cuffing his hands tightly behind his back. He was indeed owned.

"You're not listening, Samira. There's a proven connection between the cycle of solar eruptions and our urban riots—1981, 2011 and now this! The Russian heliocosmists were right. Sun spots are driving this. I have data, it all fits." Fawcett thrust his open laptop across Samira's desk, jabbing a finger at the spreadsheet on his screen, but she pushed it away, frowning over a feed from one of the surviving CCTVs.

"That's nut-job rubbish. And what could we do about it anyway? Here's what's happening in Streatham High Road." On the streaky pixellating screen two burnt-out Victorian Gothic churches faced each other across a T-junction jammed with stationary cars, their roof-racks and tailgates overloaded with luggage. The camera panned erratically high above the intersection. The audio was only a rush of white noise but Fawcett could see scuffles already breaking out and could almost lip-read the yells of road-rage invective.

For the junction was blocked by a convoy of water tanker trucks. The lead vehicle had collided with an overturned ambulance. An angry crowd was swarming all over the truck, smashing the windscreen and dragging the protesting driver from the cab. Bullet holes had perforated the underside of the tank. Men, women and children stampeded towards it, desperate to lick or suck the dripping water. A fat blonde man in shorts clambered up a ladder at the back of the next truck and forced open a valve, releasing a rainbow spray over the ecstatic mob. Droplets of water hit the camera lens as the screen went blank.

Samira was suddenly crying, to Fawcett's alarm. He tried to respond appropriately.

"Don't panic, Samira. We've got gallons of water in our tank, and we're thirty feet underground."

"My sister and her kids live half a mile from all that. I ought to try to try and reach them, bring them back here."

Karl wondered for a second if Samira actually had a sister in South London. Perhaps she'd become stir-crazy, desperate to escape from their claustrophobic hideaway and take her chances in the community.

"You told me we had a commitment to stay here and monitor the receivers."

"I'm going outside..." As she got up and bustled around the cramped bunker, grabbing at her backpack, sun-hood and dark glasses, Fawcett realised he lacked the energy to prevent her doomed expedition—and perhaps the motivation. If he had silence, solitude, a cool space to reflect, perhaps he could at least find some ultimate meaning in the crisis.

Helston didn't turn to see the captor who was pushing him hard towards another battered metal door. He staggered past a piece of grimy iron furniture, like a barbecue re-purposed as an altar, daubed with grease-spattered solar motifs. The woman deposited her fire-lance and cylinder of petrol alongside other obsolete weapons—a WW2 machine gun, two rusty shotguns propped against the wall.

"Who are you?" she hissed.

Helston began a mumbled explanation of his role with Solnet, monitoring the Zones in preparation for a mass evacuation.

"Not true, waste-man. We're going nowhere. That's what your people want. Let the garbage people burn..."

"I'm looking for Dr Raymond. He's one of our key advisers."

"Raymond..." She paused and repeated the word slowly, even reverently. She turned and shouted in that impenetrable patois. The inner door creaked open. Two Asian youths in combat gear pushed Helston inside. The taller one carried a pistol on his belt.

As his sight adapted to the gloom of the conical space, Helston could see some kind of throne, seemingly constructed from the seating of a luxury SUV. A tall black man sat there, immobile, eyes concealed by dark glasses. The youths took up their positions on either side of him, an honour guard for their emperor in his black and gold robe and golden helmet. Helston had a brief flash of an old photo depicting an African-American musician called Sun Ra, or some such name, before another image overlaid it. He tried to equate what he was seeing with recollections of the white-suited professor of cosmology he'd met in seminars decades ago.

"Doctor Raymond?"

"You are addressing Father Ray," whispered the tall bodyguard, annoyed by some breach of protocol.

"Don't you recognise me—Adam Helston?"

"Father Ray dwells in darkness!" The guard seemed outraged. "It is a blasphemy to speak of sight in his presence."

"I know you, Adam Helston..." The voice was deeper than Helston remembered, but the South London/West Indian inflections were still there. "I know Adam Helston, those clipped vowels, voiceprint of the old colonials, the old boys club-house. But you won't be part of our sound world much longer." Raymond gave a burst of guttural laughter.

"You're blind now?" Helston recalled Dr Raymond at the lectern, his fierce eye scoping the lecture room to alight on a student who might not be following his elegant equations on the white-board.

"Cataracts, my man. I could have had the surgery. But this is better for sharpening the inner vision..."

"What do you mean? What does any of this mean?" Helston waved a hand at the rough walls of the Temple, which were daubed with spray markings that might have been equations—or graffiti—before realising the futility of the gesture.

"Come on, Helston. You had pretensions to be a scientist, you know it's been a perfect storm for years—rising CO^2 emissions, ozone depletion, deforestation, all driving the global temperature rise and an increasingly fissile society. And now we have increased solar activity. Flares and sunspots. A drought in the streets. All your beloved green initiatives have been in vain. If there had been a Stalin to implement them, things might have been different—although I doubt it..."

"But what about your 'inner vision?"

"Later...." He turned and spoke in patois to his minder, who stepped down from the dais and nudged Helston towards the door. In the anteroom the guard led him to the woman in silver-foil robes. He prodded Helston in the ribs with his gun.

"Father Ray says you help Celeste on the water run. Be thankful we haven't flamed you..."

Helston panted as he struggled to push the water trolley down a rough track towards the artesian well, hidden in a circle of pine trees. The big tank wobbled on its wooden platform and the iron wheels grated on the pebbles. Celeste followed him with a hose and hand-pump.

"Keep moving, old waste-man..."

The sunlight seemed to penetrate every cell of his being, while sweat stung his eyes. He'd daubed his face and arms with cream before setting out on this quest but it could no longer protect him. He lurched down past the ring of conifers through brown ferns. The whole clearing shimmered and vibrated in the heat. Celeste was somehow ahead of him now.

Under her direction, he managed to position the trolley against the stonework of the well, while she unrolled the hose. He peered down into a mass of black sludge. Even in his near delirium he was certain any aquifer below had finally dried up.

"There's only mud, Celeste..."

She stared over the parapet in disbelief. For a second it seemed as she if was going to hit him across the face with the pump. But she hurled it into the undergrowth, screaming and sobbing, and ran off into the parched bushes. Helston slumped down on the trolley. He wondered what might happen if he returned to the Temple, alone, with an empty tank. But if he remained out here in the scorching heat, he could be dead within hours.

Samira had not been close to her sister Malika for several years now, ever since Malika's marriage to Brian, a one-time sociology academic, who had now been called up to join a reclamation gang after the closure of his university. Brian had scoffed at Malika's religious heritage and now four-old Scott and baby Amy were being raised as atheists. Perhaps her sister wanted to thumb her nose at their Muslim roots. But as Samira's electric VW arrived at their neat terrace house, those family issues felt irrelevant, melted away by the fury of the solar storm-front.

Samira paused at the front gate and glanced down the empty street. People must be sheltering in their basements, terrified of risking sunstroke and the menace of water pirates or muggers. She was glad that she had a taken a circuitous route through the back streets. Outside the air-cooled shell of the car, the heat slammed into her forehead so she hastened to the porch—to find the door unlocked.

99

She called again and again as she paced through the sauna-like living room and kitchen before risking the upstairs heat and surveying the empty bedrooms. On the stairs, a broken plastic toy robot. Perhaps Scott had dropped—or thrown it? But the children's cots were neatly made and the TV in the master bedroom was untouched. No indicators of looting. Then she saw a rubber hose dangling from the hatch in the landing ceiling and realised someone had been trying to siphon water from the tank in the roof space. Perhaps she could find further clues in Brian's study.

Brian's text-books were scattered all over the floor and the book shelves had been torn from the wall, which was now covered in tangled graffiti, a multicoloured swirl of asemic scribble, bulbous semi-vowels overlapping scratched angular quasi-consonants or mutating into serpentine creatures of fire, all crudely smeared as if executed at high speed. Yet at the centre these scrawls bordered an irregular orange disc. Across it, legible scribble: SUN TEMPLE! GO! GO!

Samira sank to the floor. Her head throbbed with the heat and the riddle of this sinister imperative desecrating the wall. She tried to imagine prim rationalist Brian inscribing his once pristine paintwork in some manic delirium. Or had the marks been left by an intruder who had coerced the family into a doomed adventure? This 'Temple' was a lunatic obsession of Adam Helston's. But she forced herself upright. There was nowhere else to go now.

Helston was finding it hard to breathe with the leather hood over his head. He struggled to remain upright and raise his voice above a whisper, dreading the next blow to his kidneys.

"Where's Celeste?"

"You raped her by the well, yes? And left her to die..."

"You lie about the water. There has always been water..."

Helston was retching with the stink of the hood. He could barely croak.

"Please, let me speak to Doctor Ray."

"You are waste, human waste. Not worthy to stand uncovered in his presence."

"I have knowledge that might help us. About the sun. But I need to know more ..." He faltered, close to collapse, his focus disrupted by the muffled chanting of Ray's disciples in the inner chamber. Their intonations rose and fell creating an hypnotic rhythm. He understood it as SUNPOWER/SUNPOWER/SUNPOWER, a mantra revolving slowly around him as he sank into unconsciousness.

Samara couldn't avoid the fires. Much of the Streatham area had been demolished to prepare for the construction of a new Cyclops Receptor Antenna. But now the rebellious inhabitants were trying to reclaim their Zone by perversely intensifying the destruction. The woods on Tooting Bec Common were ablaze, probably the work of a heat-crazed arsonist toying with a lens. She accelerated down Garrard's Road, aware that any second that one of the ancient oaks bordering the avenue could crash down, entangling her in its corona of flame. She struggled to keep the scalding wheel steady, recognising that Malika and her family might never have made it past this inferno.

Helston was trying to explain, although words kept slipping away from his swollen tongue. His tormentors had removed the hood and left him to face the unseeing gaze of Brother Ray.

"Sun spots... you mentioned... correlation between the cycles and urban unrest... if we could control these... nuclear warheads dissipate them... or shift the earth's orbit altogether... a forcefield using solar energy itself..." He knew that he was only playing for time with this gabble of crazy improvisations, even before Ray spoke.

"You have been watching too many old black and white films." The High Priest laughed. "But you have made a useful inference. You simply need to alter the terms of the equation. It is we who are controlling the sun..."

"That's insane. How can we control a star, even a minor one?"

"We live on a pan-psychic cosmos. Everything in the universe is alive and interconnected. The pulsing emanations of the solar cycle affect our moods, disrupt our social structures.

The heliocosmists in Moscow established that long ago. But our emotions, our rage and fear, our deep-rooted existential terrors act in morphic resonance with the fiery whorls and vortices of the sun, generating violent negative feedback cycles, which in turn create more solar eruptions—and so on. But perhaps not quite ad infinitum. Our fury is actually polluting the sun! We must be presented from hastening its death..."

"The heat and your blindness have confused you, Dr. Raymond.'"

"'On the contrary, they have been essential stimuli. I now know what is to be done...'"

Samira ran through the parched scrubland towards the Sun Temple. She was approaching physical and mental burn-out. Why had Malika's arch-sceptic partner abducted her nephew and niece into the furnace of this Panic Zone? The air scorched her lungs but she stumbled forward, skirting a circular clearing that sloped down towards an ancient stone well—and then almost tripped over a body of a black woman, lying sideways in the sun-bleached pine needles. She wore muddied silver robes. One claw-like hand was extended across the raw earth, as grabbing in vain for a stalk of grass, a tiny pool of moisture, but her eyes were closed.

Samira had dropped her water bottle in the frenzy of her flight and the woman seemed beyond help and it was essential to keep moving... Perhaps she could get help later. Perhaps Brian and the children were hiding in the brittle bushes, ready to lead her on a manic fire dance through blackened shrubbery towards the Temple. If only she could get in there, find some shade... The metallic sphere at its apex was now visible, reflecting a blinding glare.

Samira stopped, gripped a seared branch for support and closed her eyes for several minutes. Her head filled with an inrush of noise, rapidly increasing in volume, a babel of shouts and chants. She re-opened sore eyelids, revealing a noisy crowd gathering around the base of the structure. The headgear implied an ethnic mix from her old neighbourhood—burkas, fedoras, skull caps, turbans—even the spiked metal helmet of a huge man attired as a sun god. It was hard to see in the floating dust. Some smaller figures darted in and out, ragged boys trading in recycled plastic bottles filled with brownish grey liquid. No sign of Malika's brood. She staggered on

A rumbling noise made her turn. Two Rastas were hauling an iron wheeled trolley over the bumpy path. It carried a swaying tower of speakers and amplification equipment, together with a small generator. They didn't register her presence as they passed. Finally sinking to the ground, her limbs aching she watched them push through the crowd and set up. Within minutes she heard the throb of a heavy dub bass line and echoing fragments of vocal.

Hey man if you got the fire
I got holy smoke for your lungs
I sun system man...

The solar congregation were encircling their Temple now, like Haj pilgrims surging around the Black Stone of Mecca. Despite her pain and heat-sickness, Samira slowly dragged herself metre after metre across the fractured ground to join them. She was almost certain she could see Brian somewhere in this swirling mirage of faces, carrying Amy on his shoulders as if on a surreal post-woodland picnic. Malika must be there too, thighs moving sensuously to the pulse of the *haram* music. Her weak, reckless sister...

Samira squinted, trying to protect her eyes against the fury of the light. A figure broke away from the edge of the crowd and for a second she felt relief—before realising it was neither Malika nor Brian.

"What are you doing here, Ms Ahmed? Sent to monitor me, maybe?" Helston's voice was raw as his face, while his clothes hung in faded shreds.

"You and I need to agree a truce now, Adam. What's happening here?"

"We're here to take control, Samira. Control of the sun. You and I have our part to play."

She was too weary to resist as he took her hand and led her through the churning mass of bodies to the Temple door.

"The sun is stricken. We have poisoned its cells with the astral effluent of our hatreds, we have distorted its vortices with our spiralling desires and frustrations, we have defiled the face of the solar entity with our lust for power. We abused its energy to indulge our decadent society in the follies of consumerism. It is time for us to heal its wounds and assuage its seething rage."

Father Ray gestured to the guards holding Helston and Samira. "Take them... Take them to the Lens!"

The tall guard hustled them towards a ramshackle spiral staircase. As they tramped up the rusty iron steps, Helston stared ahead, expressionless, ignoring Samira's desperate grip on his forearm. The priests had begun chanting again, their hoarse voices echoing through the ironwork over the distant boom of the sound system beyond the Temple walls. Father Ray followed them, guiding himself with a solar-motif staff which he rapped against the stanchions of the stairway.

They arrived at a metal platform. Samira realised from the tapering walls that they were close to the apex of the conical structure. In front of them lay a wide steel grill, the size and shape of a single bed. Its blackened bars and chains were coated in small lumps and crusts of charred tissue—the source of an odour that pervaded the space and nearly forced her to vomit with revulsion and terror. Helston merely nodded as if in recognition of an appointed time and place.

Above them, the convex Lens, at least two metres in diameter. Above that, the copper globe that surmounted the whole structure and the hinge mechanism that could swing it aside, creating an aperture for sunlight to enter the Lens.

"It will soon be noon. The Sun's power will be at its zenith. We must choose an offering." Father Ray reached out and ran his fingers over Samira's cheek and neck, fondling her hair under the folds of her hijab. "The traditional victim was a virgin, of course. Are you such a virgin?'"

"I have not yet chosen a husband.'" There was no option but to admit the truth. She was beyond terror now, in a state of suspended disbelief, a kind of sleep paralysis. She already envisaged the end, hot hands forcing her wrists into manacles, the greasy bars of the sun-bed biting into her back and the moment when the cover of the Lens swung open, exposing her to the focused beam that would slowly drill a smoking hole through her body. With such intense heat, there might be no pain...

"You will be a healing incense for the Solar Spirits." Ray gestured to his enforcers. They gripped Samira by the shoulders and started pushing her down on their sacrificial altar.

"'No!" Helston lurched forward, as if awakening from a coma, and grappled with the men, forcing the younger one to trip and fall heavily. Grabbing Ray's heavy staff, Helston smashed it into the skull of his colleague, who reeled back against a corroded railing, which snapped, sending him tumbling down the stairwell. Ray, struggling to decode the noises around him, clung to Samira but flinched from a possible encounter with the spiked rays of the staff. He began shouting for help but his cries competed with the roar of the chanting.

Samira watched helplessly as Helston tugged at a chain suspended from the roof. She could hear the creak of the aperture opening but had to shut her eyes as Helston lowered himself to the altar and the blinding beam of photons was revealed, a laser-like radiance already penetrating his heart, but appearing to emanate from it.

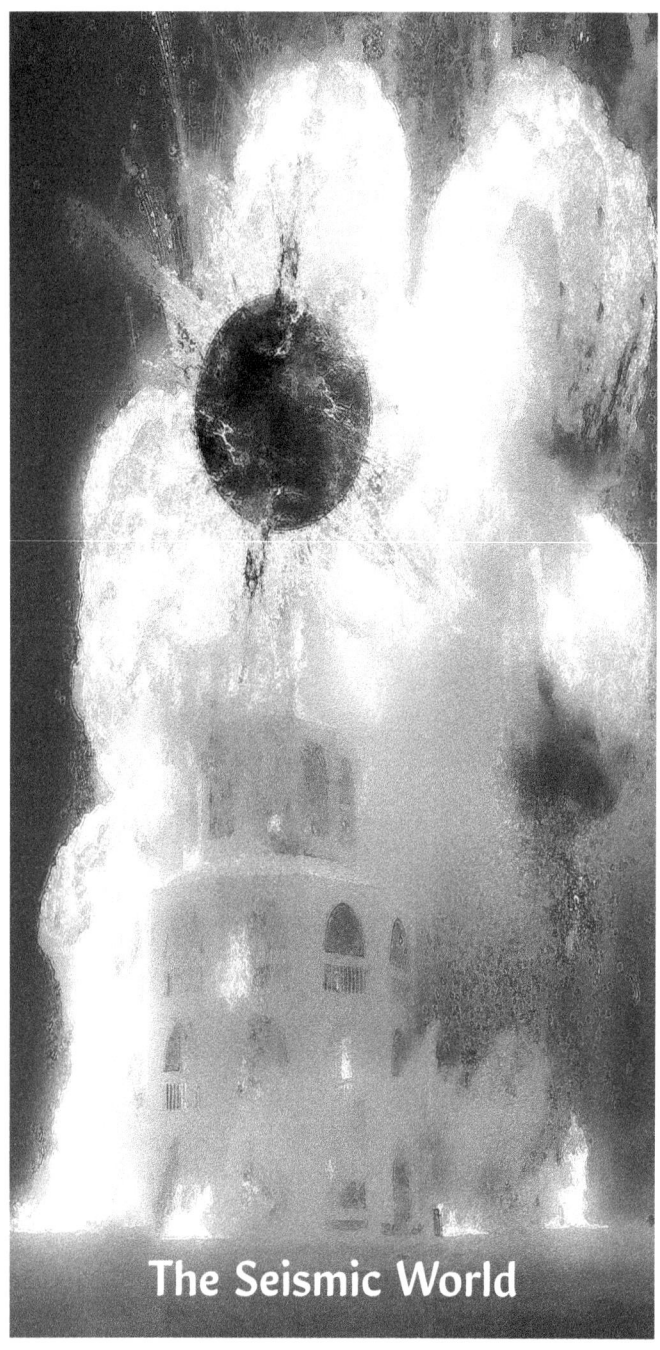

The Seismic World

The dinghy tossed and yawed in the rolling waves, and for a moment Dr. Langham wondered if the refugees were going to make it. He gripped the railing of the observation post as he squinted through cloudy binoculars. The tiny overcrowded vessel was only two hundred yards from the edge of Platform One but it could so easily capsize.

To Langham's relief a patrol boat had already spotted them. Two marines loud-hailed the dark-skinned man in a wet-suit at the tiller of the dinghy's outboard motor. They were signalling him to manoeuvre closer and threw out a line to begin the precarious business of transferring his passengers to the larger craft.

Langham could now study the migrants—at least two dozen —as they slowly made the dangerous transfer into the swaying patrol boat, all apparently exhausted, several minus life-jackets and some clearly injured. But they were, as a demographic, much as he expected, mostly white but with a scattering of darker faces. Some men wore muddy hi-viz tabards, there were women and small children huddled in metallic foil blankets and indeterminate figures swathed in grubby bandages—probably from fractures or burns. There would certainly be work for him, more than enough to justify his ration allotment, although the Platform surgery was currently running low on dressings and anaesthetics. But even before triage, the new arrivals would have to be processed, via the usual debriefing with Commander Brewer's security team, who would assess the skills and resources they might bring to Platform One.

It began to drizzle. He turned up the hood of his precious old anorak and swung away from the railing to walk carefully across the slippery plating of the empty top deck, where the faded yellow mandala identifying the heli-port was still kept clear, although it had been three years since a coast guard chopper had landed. Gulls soared and swooped under the greyish-brown overcast, a permanent skyscape now across the Channel. He could taste dust in the wind, metallic grit.

Arriving at the hatch to the central stairwell, he stepped quickly down to Level C and hurried along narrow corridors. The passages were cluttered with boxes of salvaged tinned foods while an overhead loudspeaker played ancient top-40 hits, a morale-raising strategy that Langham found depressing, as if he were trapped in the aisles of some dystopian supermarket. He finally pulled open a bulkhead door stencilled FORECASTING SECTION.

"This isn't a good time, Richard." Joanna Graham didn't look up, focusing instead on the waveforms flickering across a desktop monitor. "We keep losing the feed from our main hydrophone. I've no idea what's going on down there."

"Platform Two at Dogger Bank might have some info."

"You know as well as I do that we haven't heard from Dogger Bank in three weeks. It's something we're not supposed to talk about."

Langham cursed himself for his lack of diplomacy. Joanna was so neurotic about complying with Commander Brewer's directives.

"Can't you collate data from the land stations and extrapolate from that?"

"We've lost so many sensors. Since Geo-Survey in Edinburgh went down, I only get random readings. There was a 3.2 at a depth of 9 klicks around Bangor last night and a 2.3 at a depth of 6 centred on Hereford but I'm sure there have been more. Maybe something bigger near Dartford."

Langham tried to visualise the locations—a ruptured shopping precinct, maybe a sagging tower block and mountains of rubble hindering token rescue efforts, perhaps even smoking crevices bubbling with lava. There was no national TV coverage now, one had to rely on the hazy imagery captured on survivors' phones. Even one's memory of the mainland was uncertain.

"Dartford—isn't that in Kent? There could be a tidal surge along the coast."

"The Thames estuary has probably become a lake. Maybe the new arrivals can fill you in. Isn't that where you should heading?" She got up abruptly. Crossing to a wall map she began pressing pins into a geography already punctured with hundreds of red markings.

As Langham murmured a farewell, his gaze lingered on the line of her neck, her mane of dark hair and the curve of her

108

body under a heavy jersey and dungarees. But in the spartan dormitory regime of Platform One there were few opportunities for privacy or sexual entanglement. And, as Brewer was fond of telling his crew, work kept one grounded.

The Great Seismic Shift, as it became known, had begun over a decade ago, as subterranean activity increased along the Pacific fault lines running under Japan, Indonesia and the Philippines, where earthquakes had occurred since records began. The defining moment was probably the death of nearly fifty three thousand people following a massive tectonic plate shift just off the Bay of Manila. Yet even this horror was at first viewed as part of an ongoing historical narrative that could be somehow mediated and rationalised. When that was followed by a huge volcanic eruption on the island of Santorini in the Aegean and a series of quakes and mini-tsunamis near Naples and around Venice—in which the city was finally submerged—questions were raised in the UN and other NGO bodies, only leading to a consensus that little could be done except increase budgets for aid and rescue services while reviewing building regulations in vulnerable zones.

In the following eighteen months the "vulnerable zones" came to include whole swathes of the USA and Northern Europe. In the UK, which normally saw only a few score of minor tremors per year, there were major incidents like the sudden crash, at peak commuting time, of West London's Chiswick flyover and the total collapse of the North Terminal at Gatwick Airport, followed by innumerable fissured roads and demolished houses across the whole country from Dundee to St Ives. Fatalities quickly rose from the hundreds to the hundreds of thousands as emergency services were overwhelmed and the country's infrastructure began, literally, to crumble. Amid this chaos, a beleaguered government in the COBRA bunker under Whitehall watched pixellated footage of the San Andreas Fault calamity, as Los Angeles slid inexorably into the ocean.

So began the desperate initiative of the Platforms. It was clearly imperative to create a secure national command centre that would be unaffected by the worsening geological situation. Thus Britain needed a marine-based equivalent of the old Cold War RSGs, the Regional Seats of Government. The nation's military and economic resources were concentrated on building a group of floating islands around the coast of the British Isles. The largest, Platform One, ten miles off the Sussex coast, generated its own power, both nuclear and wind-driven, and hosted its own desalination plant and trawler docks, as well as pens for landing craft and patrol vessels. It supported a population of over a thousand, comprising soldiers, fishermen, scientists, engineers and displaced bureaucrats. There was only sporadic contact with shattered regimes in Paris and Brussels. In one sense, Britannia continued to rule the waves.

"OK, Langham, what have we got here?" Commander Jack Brewer glanced around the low ceilinged space that functioned as an emergency ward. Half a dozen refugees sprawled on the beds, two of them hooked to saline drips. A sergeant shouldering a carbine stood by the door, as if to prevent them escaping.

The lower body of an elderly man on the nearest gurney was wrapped in grubby blood stained dressings. His face was scorched and blackened, his eyes were closed and he was breathing erratically.

"I'm afraid I couldn't do much for this one. Except morphine." Langham regretted the admission but he'd learned there was no point in prevaricating with the Commander, a stocky bearded figure, reputedly ex-Marine, terse and tight-lipped.

"Lava burns?" The question was purely a formality. Brewer had overseen Langham's often futile attempts to treat survivors after previous quakes and eruptions. "No worries. I know opiate supplies are low. Sergeant Furey will process him. Now do you have any walking wounded? Have you done their stats?"

Langham handed the Commander a clip board, but before he could flip through it a woman's voice called from a bed at the far end.

"Just give me a fucking brace for my leg. And get me

out of here." She grimaced as she levered herself upright and groped for a cup of water on the bedside table. Langham was struck by her rain-smeared kohl makeup, her corona of spiky greenish hair and worn leather jacket. She was early forties, her inflections were nasal, urban. *Post-punk posing as post apocalyptic—Brewer will not be impressed* thought Langham.

"So where do you think you're going? Do you want us to throw you back into the English Channel? Or do you want to go with him?" Brewer gestured with his thumb towards the bandaged figure on the trolley. But the woman stared him down.

Sensing a confrontation, Langham intervened. "Perhaps the lady could remind us of her name and boarding status."

"Lou Axton. Your zombie boys told me I was C1. What's that all about?" Langham had a sudden flash of recall, a clip from distant pre-Seismic TV news: *performance artist/activist Louise Axton creates live installation at fracking site.* Dim image of a muddy half-naked figure writhing in a trench…

"Catering duties for you, Ms Axton. Unless you'd prefer to work in the Staff Recreation Area. It's a job you could do lying down." Brewer allowed himself a faint smirk.

Langham was anxious to forestall a riposte from Axton that would make her position with Brewer even more uncertain. Her vitality triggered both unease and curiosity. So many of the patients he'd treated had been traumatised into total passivity.

"I could use an assistant, Commander. We need to keep track of our drug inventory and the patient logs." The request might appeal to Brewer's obsession with maintaining order.

"You better make it work, Dr. Langham. We'll review the situation in a week." Brewer was already impatient. "Just get the rest of these people patched up for a labour detail. I've got a Food Supply meeting in five minutes." He strode off, followed by the sergeant wheeling out the terminal patient.

Langham began treating Louise Axton's ankle, which was cut and badly bruised but not broken. She winced and looked up suspiciously as he adjusted the dressing.

"I'm not Recreation fodder, Doctor, if that's what you were hoping."

Langham, groping in his trouser pocket for paracetamol tablets, ignored the probe. He was suddenly aware of his exhaustion and hunger. He could only make conversation on auto-pilot.

"So where was it? The quake?"

"Around what was left of Dartford, near the Bluewater Centre. A fissure, a hot one. It got old Arthur before he could run..." She began shaking and sobbing. There was no point in telling her that Sergeant Furey was about to dispatch Arthur with a pistol shot and send his body bag over the side.

In the half-light of the dormitory Langham found it impossible to sleep. Barnett, the engineer in the next cubicle, a former oil-rig worker, was muttering incoherently, tossing and turning in uneasy dreams.

In desperation Langham decided to seek distraction in his portable radio. He plugged in earphones and began his nightly sweep through the FM and AM bands. The Top 40 station that was piped through the Platform's tannoy system was blaring away as usual, and Langham briefly wondered if it was being transmitted from a ship further up the Channel. Yet there were no announcements or station IDs, so he could only presume the programming was automated on a loop. He found intermittent bursts of what might have been Urdu on one of the old BBC wavelengths, but otherwise he was dialling through waves of static and crackle. He eventually turned off to conserve the batteries. Thankfully Barnett had fallen silent at last.

He groped for the faded photo under his pillow— another late night ritual. The wedding picture with Anna was almost bleached, but he could still study her faint smile and recognise the jaunty posture of this striking young woman in a white trouser suit. He stared through the scratched perspex of the frame at the grinning mask of a previous self which had yet to lose its curls of black hair and sharply defined bone structure. In the chaos of his transfer to the Platform he'd lost the phone containing her excited message from the airport at Seattle, where she'd just arrived to deliver a keynote speech at that conference on autism. Then, after the West

Coast calamity, he heard nothing—for hours that became days, then months.

Her death was only one among millions yet he was still appalled by its arbitrary cruelty and mystery. For no-one had yet found a definitive explanation for this global catastrophe. Joanna Graham had briskly dismissed the once-fashionable theory of lunar influenced geological "earth tides" when he'd first mentioned it, while Brewer discouraged speculation about ultimate causes, preferring to concentrate minds on the practicalities of survival. Langham had no background in astrophysics or geology—his medical training had originally been intended as a route to practising psychiatry—but he wondered if solar magnetic storms might have affected the Earth's metallic core.

Louise Axton, of course, had all the answers. That afternoon, as she hobbled around the pharmacy stockroom, she'd let him know that world-wide fracking was responsible for the Shift. "The Patriarchy carves up Mother Earth, so what do we get? This is Gaia's rebellion, she's shaking us off, it's her dance of defiance. I was telling everyone for years in my art, my interventions. Now look where we are." Langham didn't have the energy to engage and was trying to make sense of his scribbled surgery notes. But he somehow respected her bloody mindedness and the pluck that had brought her on this dangerous voyage. He imagined her in her bunk in the women's quarters, keeping Jo Graham awake with fervent eco-centric diatribes.

He flipped open one of the few paperbacks he'd salvaged, an old psychology text: *Collective earthquake dreams can indicate neurotic problems at a collective scale in the complex of fulfilment of aggressive instincts*. A bizarre synchronicity. But he was too tired to cope with psychiatric jargon. He let the book fall to the floor and turned over in his bunk as Platform One swayed and rolled with the incessant motion of the waves.

Langham was late for the morning meeting in the mess room. He tried to slip in unobtrusively at the back but couldn't avoid a hostile glance from Brewer who stood at the far end, gesturing with a pointer at a large map of southern England.

"...the importance of this expedition. It's not only the objective of replenishing supplies and salvaging materials. There's a bigger issue at stake—as our guest Mr Anwar Zahid will tell us."

Langham was surprised to see the bearded Asian dinghy pilot sitting among Brewer's uniformed lieutenants, alongside Barnett and the other team leaders. He strode confidently to the front. Langham recognised a strong East London accent.

"Maybe you lot think that I've made the crossing just to find bed and breakfast. But I'm here on a mission. There are still communities over there. Brothers and sisters are struggling but they're trying to reach out."

Langham recalled the fragments he'd picked out on his radio—cries for assistance or territorial proclamations?

"They could use your help. And you can't be stuck here for ever. What was the idea of the Platforms? To take back control of the mainland, to re-build a working economy—"

Barnett, in the front row, snorted with laughter. "Economy! What fucking planet are you living on, mate? Scavenge and barter—that's all we've got!"

Brewer glared at him. "Negative talk means you lose special ration privileges, Barnett. Listen to the man!" Barnett scowled but subsided.

Zaheed pointed to the map. "Before we quit Dartford, I was getting signals from the London orbital zone. They've got some kind of safe space there, a settlement almost. You can link up, share info. We can re-colonise the land..."

Jo Graham raised a hand. "He could be on to something, Commander. We haven't had any big readings from that area recently."

"You mean we're going to get some real action, sir?" Private Burton couldn't hide his excitement. There was a sudden buzz in the room, a collective energy that Langham had not witnessed for months.

Brewer signalled for silence. "You will have a full briefing tomorrow. In the meantime I expect Forecasting to prepare a projection of likely tremor areas. Dismiss!"

While they filed out, the younger soldiers and technicians clearly enthused by this unexpected announcement, Dr. Langham wondered how much Louise Axton had paid the dinghy pilot for her crossing. What other motivation could Zahid have for that risky venture and this potentially dangerous voyage into a devastated interior? As he pondered, Brewer came over and slapped him on the shoulder. "Don't think you can stay behind doling out pills, Langham. England expects every man et cetera..."

Five days later, Langham and Axton clung to the deck of LCT 7074, a huge rusty D-Day Landing Craft, as it approached Cooden Beach through early morning mist. Nearly two hundred feet in length, it had originally been built to land ten tanks and a complement of soldiers in Normandy in 1944.

"History's full of ironies, isn't it," shouted Langham over the throb of diesel engines. "This is one of the sites where the Germans intended to land in 1940."

But the reference seemed lost on Louise, who was staring suspiciously at a squat arachnoid vehicle on a low trailer at the front of the craft.

"That evil-looking thing gives me the creeps. It's the eight legs."

"Pirated American technology. Good for scrambling through the rubble. You better get used to it. We'll need it to reconnoitre." Langham tried to be buoyant but he knew that their main cargo, three Bulldog caterpillar-tracked armoured personnel carriers, might struggle in the terrain.

As the bow of the landing craft entered the shallows, Brewer barked orders through a megaphone. While the engines of the personnel carriers growled into life the forward ramp slowly creaked open. Louise ran down and began to wade into the rippling waves like a child on holiday but Langham pulled her back to where the Spider crouched on its metallic limbs. He hustled her inside the control pod and flicked a switch on the dashboard.

"Don't worry, I'm used to these." A lie. He'd only driven a Spider once, as emergency medic after the Gatwick disaster, an endless night of blood and mud. But the controls were intuitive and he wanted to avoid travelling with Furey's men in the Bulldogs. Joanna could probably fend for herself, protected by her upper class hauteur from the banter of the squaddies, but he surely had a duty of care to his former patient.

Motors hummed as the Spider flexed its legs, rose from its mounting, and began a crabwise walk down the gangway to the pebbled beach. The Bulldogs followed, their tracks clanking down the ramp.

A few minutes later Brewer ordered everyone to leave their vehicles for a briefing. Langham stepped warily over stones, driftwood and slivers of plastic. It had been a long time since he had walked on land and his body was already anticipating some phantom tremor, a shiver in the ground that presaged disaster. The top of the beach was bordered by a bank of rubble, the remains of bungalows or bathing huts. Brewer was pointing beyond this while Zahid unrolled a crumpled map. Langham was surprised when the former "refugee", now wearing military fatigues, addressed the group instead of the Commander.

"On the far side we'll find what's left of the railway and beyond that what used to be the A259 route eastward to Bexhill and Hastings. We have to go east because everything west, from Brighton up to Crawley is blocked. So we're turning north at Hastings to find a route up the A21 towards the Orbital Zone. Our objective is Tunbridge Wells by dusk."

"The Earth energies are all wrong..." Louise whispered to herself. "We lost the ley of the land. This is going nowhere." Langham ignored her pseudo-profundities. Whatever Zahid and Brewer were intending, his only option on this unstable planet was to keep moving.

As the twilight deepened, Brewer stood up in the hatch of the lead Bulldog and flagged the convoy to a halt. Langham struggled to hear his instructions over the fading whine of the Spider's electrics but soldiers were already hauling out inflatable bell tents to set up an encampment. They'd stopped at a road junction outside the skewed facade of a motel, where a crooked sign still promised "Traditional Fayre." The convenience store at the service station around the corner was a burned-out shell. However the pumps looked intact and Furey was leading a small group over to scout for diesel. Louise had fallen asleep.

It had taken them all day to reach the fractured tarmac of this former A-road on the north side of Hastings—so much for Zahid's "objective". All the way from Bexhill through St Leonards and onwards, repeated incursions of the sea had washed away whole stretches of the promenade and forced them to constantly reverse and re-route through a labyrinth of ruined streets. Avenues had become cul-de-sacs, punctured with huge sink-holes or piled with fragmented brickwork and rusting salvage equipment. Langham became tasked with reconnaissance, manipulating the legs of the Spider to stagger over broken beams or fallen pillars and check the ground ahead. At one point they became blocked in both directions by tumbling masonry and spent an hour excavating a path around the wreckage of a retirement home, now a pyre of brickwork, twisted walking frames and crushed mobility buggies. Despite his compassion fatigue, Langham was still compelled to wonder what skeletal remains were trapped within this asymmetric pyramid. At St Leonards they had encountered the vast white bulk of an Art Deco apartment block, tilted at a forty-five degree angle. It loomed over them like an ocean liner run aground, ready to collapse at the slightest tremor. The column had inched past, one vehicle at a time, seconds before the entire building roared down in a cyclone of dust and debris.

Louise woke up as Langham climbed out of the Spider pod. She stumbled down beside him, took the water bottle that he offered and drank greedily.

"So here I am, still in the dead zone. Like an extra in an old zombie movie."

"Everywhere's a dead zone, Louise. But this area would have been cleared years ago. I expect there's a mass grave site near here."

"You can sense it. The ghost of the smell. The smell of the ghosts..." She zipped up her jacket. "Did you know that hauntings can make the temperature go down? We ought to be living in the fucking ice age."

Before Langham could attempt a reply Zahid appeared from behind the nearest Bulldog. He smiled as he gripped Langham's hand.

"You did good stuff today Doc, got us safe through some dodgy bits. Commander's well impressed."

"Thanks—but are we really going to make it all the way to the Orbital?"

"No worries, we'll get there. And you'll get your medical supplies. They tell me there's a hospital at Pembury that's sort of standing, *inshallah!*" He laughed as he walked away to join Brewer by the lead vehicle.

Inshallah—God Willing. Langham wondered how Zahid reconciled the alleged benevolence of his deity with the global suffering of the Shift. He turned to Louise.

"He seems to know everything, Lou. What can you tell me about him?"

"I was in this camp with Arthur and the others, we got quaked and were looking for a safe space. He turned up, said he could get a boat on the coast—you know the rest..."

"So how did you pay him?" Weapons or sex were common currencies. He couldn't see Louise Axton engaging in such transactions.

"He wouldn't take anything. Said it was *zakat*—charity. Part of his mission."

"What mission?"

"No idea, Doctor. I guess that we all need a mythology to keep us going." She glanced at Sergeant Furey's men pitching

their line of tents in the deepening gloom. "Better get on with our luxury accommodation."

They quickly inflated their tent and unrolled the sleeping bags in silence. Langham hoped that Brewer had arranged a reliable watch rota. Packs of dogs or feral road-men could be prowling. And there was always the random tremor.

But Louise presented a semblance of calm as she rolled into her bag and turned off her torch. "I expect you'd rather share with classy Joanna—enjoying a cosy catastrophe together and feeling the earth move?" She laughed caustically. "But we're together for the long haul, Doctor..."

It was early evening when they arrived at the hospital. Long sections of the main road had been relatively clear, and the Bulldogs had coped easily, crushing abandoned vehicles and uprooted trees. Although the building's plastic cladding had fallen like torn petals and jagged cracks had spread across its concrete buttresses, it remained upright at ninety degrees. They nevertheless stopped on the far side of the car park, where nettles and small bushes poked through the asphalt and an ambulance sat on sagging tyres. It was covered in sprawling graffiti—SHAKE BABY SHAKE!

Louise pointed at a window on the first floor. "I'm sure that's a light!"

Langham scanned the frontage. Was the artist projecting an image from her own feverish imagination? Or was it as elusive as that sudden blip of light that was supposed to precede an earthquake, according to urban lore?

"Could be visiting time on the wards, Doc. Or you might be able to pick up your prescription." Zahid was jogging his elbow. "I'm up for it if you are."

"No-one is going in without back-up." Brewer strode over to take charge, pushing Zahid aside. "Furey and three privates will lead, locked and loaded."

A few minutes later the group stepped through the broken glass of the entrance lobby, past the overturned chairs and trolleys of a deserted A&E department.

"The wounded have gone for a walk..." Louise ran a finger

through the dust covering a bench. Langham ignored her as they stalked down the corridors scoping out the signage with their torches. When they approached the pharmacy, Private Burton steadied his revolver with both hands, as he'd learned from old VHS police dramas, and peered through the doors before beckoning Langham and Axton inside. As the Doctor feared, it had been ransacked, shelves overturned or torn from the wall in a manic frenzy. Empty packets littered the floor.

"Tough shit, Doc." Zahid was laconic, almost amused.

They climbed the stairs to the first floor. The first ward was empty—even the beds had been dismantled, stained mattresses were stacked in random heaps—but as they passed the entrance to Intensive Care, Langham was convinced he could hear shuffling noises and a faint keening sound.

"There's some kind of animal in there..."

"That's laughter, Doc. It's a welcoming party." Zahid gripped Langham's elbow. "They're waiting for you to do your rounds."

The doors flew back and a long-haired grizzled man in filthy surgical scrubs lurched out, giggling as he locked eyes with Langham. He held a scalpel at arm's length in both hands, moving it from side to side as if dowsing for the blood that had long ago dried on the tiled floor.

"Where do we make the incision? The planet's fibrillating, we've got to get to the heart of it." As the psychic surgeon lunged towards Louise, Burton pistol-whipped his jaw and he fell to the floor, grunting with pain.

Suddenly Langham was gagging on a stench of urine and faeces as they became encircled by a wailing mob, mostly elderly men and women cloaked in torn bedsheets, staggering like disintegrating mummies. An obese bald man in a nurse's tunic and skirt, legs bulging in frayed black stockings, grabbed Langham by the collar and shrieked into his ear.

"Carry on, Doctor! You got to carry on. Matron's orders!"

Langham was momentarily confused, recalling those old debates about gender. Then he shook off Matron's grip and shouted back to Furey. "We must at least try!"

The sergeant shook his head but Langham and Zahid were already advancing into the ward. Smoky candlelight revealed a

120

shambolic nest of partitions improvised with broken cabinets or stacks of black garbage bags as Burton's boots crunched across discarded syringes. Langham heard a female voice mumbling behind one of the cubicles.

"Leave my tin alone... it's my tin..."

He had witnessed deprivation so many times but this terminal misery undermined his defences.

"There must be something we can do. Where are the staff?"

Zahid pointed to a faded poster over the nurses' station. STAFF EVACUATION PLAN/PHASE 1. "Looks like some manager screwed up and left a few oldies behind to self-medicate. PTSD cases. It's a mental hospital now."

"They're possessed," murmured Lou Axton. "The Earth Spirits have got them, got them shaking all over. I can feel it..." She sat on the floor, fingering fragments of glass and china into a rough mosaic.

Matron was pawing at Langham's sleeve. "You've got to come quickly, Doctor, we need a diagnosis." The fat man shoved him into an igloo of rubbish where a figure lay curled on an airbed. Langham knew immediately from the stench that the patient had been dead for days and slowly shook his head. Matron burst into theatrical tears.

"But there must be alternative ways—natural treatments—like essiac tea, crystals..."

Langham gave up. He left the cubicle and turned to Zahid. "I'm afraid we're done here."

"That's the problem with you doctors and your scientism, you're stuck in your rationalist dogmas. I can help these people. My art therapy—" Louise Axton paused in her work of bricolage. "Oh my God!... Can't you feel it?"

Her mosaic had started vibrating. Glass splinters were dancing across the floor. A dead fluorescent tube fell from the ceiling, where cracks began spreading across the plasterwork.

"Everybody into bed! Now! Now!" Matron was trying to push patients towards their cubicles but they milled around helplessly, moaning and shivering in an erratic widdershins dance. Langham was transfixed by the horror of this insane coven, even as trolleys and tables began to slide around him.

Zahid dragged at his sleeve. "Come on, Doctor. Let's get out of here!"

"We can't just leave them..." But Louise's outrage was silenced by an avalanche of plaster at the far end of the ward.

They ran for the stairs. Flashes of torchlight revealed handrails buckling into a warped expressionist geometry as they tumbled down. Langham tripped, slamming his head against the wall while the soldiers stampeded over him. Zahid pulled him upright and steadied him against the rippling metalwork of the staircase. He scrambled down the final flight half-blinded by pain, blood and clouds of dust. The floor of the exit lobby seemed to swell and heave under him, a turbulent ocean of soiled carpet tiles. He was sick with vertigo. But somehow they reached the outside and kept running.

"Bastards!" Louise was screaming into the raw night air, over the din of diesel engines and the clatter of caterpillar tracks. Brewer's Bulldog was already reversing, the Commander standing up in the top hatch to order a tactical retreat, while Furey, Burton and their comrades scrabbled for handholds on the second machine, which started rumbling towards the car park exit, headlights blazing.

Zahid cursed and ran after the departing vehicles. Langham, still dazed, wasn't sure if he was intending to stop them or catch a ride. The first Bulldog smashed through the flimsy exit barriers but the second one, in avoiding the derelict ambulance, side-swiped the Spider, crumpling two of its legs and shattering the perspex of the control pod. As the tank suddenly changed direction, Furey lost his grip and fell beneath the massive cleats of the tracks, his cry lost in the roar of the motors and a deeper almost sub-sonic vibration.

The ground shook. The hospital slid down vertically, as neatly as if it had been demolished with precision charges. Across the car park a huge chasm opened, at least thirty feet deep, exposing jumbled strata of asphalt, clay, concrete, the detritus of broken sewers and torn cabling. For the ground seemed to be slitting itself apart in a giant post-mortem autopsy. Commander Brewer's vehicle teetered on the edge, swaying back and forth, then plunged down into the darkness. The other carrier, moving forward again, lost traction as the aperture widened and rolled over into the cavity, which subsided in a vast landslide of rubble, obliterating both men and machines.

For a long time Langham lay spreadeagled face down on the concrete, body convulsing with each after-shock. He was vaguely aware of Louise and Zahid nearby. For a while she was crying and Zahid was muttering in Arabic, praying perhaps.

As dawn broke he staggered upright. The remaining Bulldog, parked some distance away, seemed undamaged. It would contain food, water and above all a radio for contacting Platform One and updating Deputy Commander McCulloch about the debacle. The expedition had failed and the only option was to return, whatever Zahid and Louise Axton might think. Shivering, he stepped around them as they slept on the broken ground and hurried past the ruptured abdomen of the Spider, before taking an elaborate detour between the rows of rusting cars, to avoid seeing the chasm and its contents.

He hesitated as he approached the personnel carrier. Perhaps some of Brewer's men had been left behind and lay in wait, ready to eliminate inconvenient civilians. But he was beyond paranoia now and grabbed the handle of the heavy rear door.

Joanna Graham was crouching on the floor amidst a pile of ration packs. Her reddened eyes stared straight through him but her lips were moving soundlessly. She was tearing her seismographic charts into neat tiny squares. At last she registered his presence.

"They're dead, aren't they? Brewer and the rest."

He nodded.

"It's not surprising they abandoned me. I'm useless." She flicked a lock of hair away and brushed the torn paperwork aside.

"You've said yourself forecasting's not an exact science."

"Science may not be the answer, Richard. I think at some level we really get off on this. Perhaps our mass neuroses and collective traumas from the aftermath of the Shift are actually the causes of it..."

Langham didn't reply. He sat down in front of the military radio console and soon realised that he had no idea how to use it. Joanna had returned to sorting her fragments, as if piecing them together again might reveal an underlying code that could ensure their safe passage. He tore open a ration pack and offered her a cereal bar but she ignored him. He ate slowly, remembering that he'd given his water flask to Louise, before drifting off to sleep again.

In his dream he was trapped in a vast ark, a floating steel and concrete island adrift on a dark torrent heading for a great waterfall at the rim of the Earth. He was part of a mass choir roaring in chorus, which segued into a deafening blast of white noise.

Louise Axton shook him awake. Zahid was crouching over the radio, adjusting volume and frequency dials.

"Unbelievable, man! No signal from your Platform One. I've been trying for half an hour." He switched off the transmitter and swigged from a dented can of energy drink.

"It must be a temporary malfunction." Joanna looked to Langham for reassurance. He shrugged. It was hard to believe that the Platform might be in difficulty, but the foundations of everyday existence were constantly drifting.

"We're fucked!" Louise exploded. "We're totally fucked." She swung a wild punch at Zahid, which he blocked with one hand. "You promised me safe passage to the Platform, then this Orbital utopia but here we are in the fucking terminal zones, more at risk than we were in Dartford."

"No worries sister. We got fuel, food. Even got kit." He gestured at the rifles and ammunition boxes stacked alongside him. "We're still on track for the Orbital. Onwards and upwards." Louise slumped down on the bench as Zahid pulled himself up into the cockpit. "I can drive this, no problem." Langham wondered where Zahid had acquired this easy familiarity with military hardware—perhaps vacationing long ago in some Middle Eastern theatre of war? He'd already assumed command.

"OK, people. We leave at nine hundred hours."

The motorway seemed endless, an erratic orbit around the vast black hole of London, where entire districts had been sucked into oblivion. They had been forced to take a lengthy detour around Reigate, grinding through the ruins of a four-level flyover collapse. Once back on course, they had to negotiate narrow lanes that were nearly blocked with overturned lorries and squeeze past the burnt-out hulks of refugee coaches. But Zahid remained unfazed, his optimism reinforced by the discovery of a tanker full of diesel fuel standing almost intact in the car park at Cobham Services. Langham could hear him declaiming in Arabic as they lurched up a slip road for yet another segment of the journey. The two women slept but Langham's brain was numbed by the incessant noise and vibration. He felt trapped in a metallic prison, subjected to sophisticated sleep deprivation techniques.

An hour passed as they traversed the obstacle course of this broken concrete desert. And then they stopped, abruptly. He could hear Zahid talking up in the cockpit, voices shouting back. The front hatch opened and a figure in a burka peered in, training her pistol at Langham's head.

"It's cool, Doc. Just a check point. Give her the gear." Langham slowly handed her the assault rifles, one by one. "You're safe now. Welcome to the People's Anglo-Islamic Republic. Take a good look." Zahid dragged him up into the commander's hatchway before resuming the driving seat. "This is the future..."

The Bulldog roared into life and began clattering down a bumpy but serviceable high street.

At little stalls along the road women in hijabs were busy buying and selling bread or vegetables. A few waved and for a second Langham felt like a general heading a victory parade into a liberated city. They passed a long white building decorated in green bunting with a crescent flag flying from the roof. Langham caught sight of a notice almost hidden by the hedge: SHEPPERTON VILLAGE HALL.

Zahid was eager to explain. "When the Shift started, the community started shifting too, out of Hounslow and West London. The bros knew Shepperton was a low quake area where we could settle. Most of the old gammons had done a runner." They passed a supermarket, battered but nevertheless functioning now as some kind of slaughterhouse, and then parades of shops, even a cafe where young men sat outside laughing and smoking shika pipes.

Zahid pulled up at an intersection. "Before we meet the Caliph, I got to show you something. A bit out of our way but never mind." They entered a long residential street of small semi-detached houses. Here minor tremors had left their marks—an overturned shed, shattered tiles, a fallen fence, cracked glazing in a yellow front door. The Bulldog nosed through the remains of some kind of barricade, improvised from rubbish bins.

"Don't think we're not multicultural. Check this out!" They halted outside a double-fronted building with picnic tables on the forecourt. Union Jacks hung from the upper windows and a St George's Cross banner stretched across the doorway. Langham was looking at a British pub, an institution from another life. An elderly white man in a cardigan emerged, looking up anxiously at this massive military machine.

"Don't worry, grand-dad," yelled Zahid. "We're not your neighbourhood *mutawa*. Just passing by." The old man still looked uneasy as he scuttled back inside. "They brew their own alcohol, you know. Strictly *haram* of course but the Caliph knows when to turn a blind eye. They need a little enclave. Got to keep some of them on side, see?"

"You want me on side, then?"

"Yeah, we always need good doctors."

"And acquiring all the Bulldogs and the hardware, that was part of the plan too? So your people would have taken out Brewer and the rest at the first opportunity?"

"Easy, man. The Caliph always negotiates first. Anyway they got quaked. So it became Plan B."

"So Lou Axton and Joanna become part of the Caliph's harem—is that included in Plan B?" He knew at once it was a cheap jibe, prompted by his own proprietary instincts towards the women.

"Hey, no stereotyping now. They will find good husbands. Anyway, we have more important stuff to do than shagging. Time for you to get educated..."

Zahid gunned the engine and pulled hard on the right track

lever, spinning the Bulldog through one hundred and eighty degrees in a shower of crumbling tarmac before heading for the administrative hub of the People's Anglo-Islamic Republic.

"Allah sometimes gives the earth permission to breathe, which brings these upheavals. And indeed He has power to send torment on you from under your feet. Our scholars agree on this. But our *umma* has survived through our repentance, hard work and our strong family bonds."

The Caliph, imposing in dark glasses and a flowing white *thobe*, smiled as he handed Joanna and Louise glasses of mint tea. They sat on cushions inside his capacious tent. Zahid radiated pride at having arranged this introduction although Langham remained uneasy. He sensed a severe resolve underlying their host's geniality.

"As I completed my PhD in physics at Cambridge I began to appreciate the full beauty of Allah's creation—but realised also its complexity, its paradoxical nature. Through the painful challenges of the Shift, He has given us an opportunity to earn merit through helping others, to transcend our petty weaknesses in true *jihad*, to unearth new skills and discover new wonders."

"Wonders? All you people wanted to discover was oil. Your god's an earth-rapist..." Louise's truculence alarmed Langham.

The Caliph frowned. "Blasphemy does not become you, sister—especially when you have been offered our hospitality. Perhaps you would prefer to take your chances elsewhere?" Zahid half-rose, taking her arm to escort her out, but the Caliph motioned him to sit.

Joanna broke the silence. "As a fellow-scientist, I'd really like to know your theories about the physical causes of the Shift."

"Theory is best demonstrated through experiment. Come with me. Yes, you too, Ms Axton. And our wise Doctor."

Zahid drew back the tent flap, revealing the rolling grasslands of Sunbury Golf Club. In the distance, beyond a line of trees, Langham noticed a complex of low windowless buildings surmounted by a tall chimney.

"Ah, the council recycling plant with the incinerator.

Before we established the *umma* there were many cremations there, a sacrilegious practice. But enough of that." The Caliph steered them in the opposite direction. Most of the greens and fairways had been repurposed as allotments where young men in white skullcaps laboured over potatoes and cabbages under a grey sky. They passed the clubhouse, in the process of being converted into a greenhouse, and skirted a small pond, now a sink of mud holding a tangle of shredded metal, perhaps the detritus of a foiled aerial attack by the secular authorities. Langham wondered how long this improvised micro-state could survive.

"Don't hang about, Doc. We're almost there. This is gonna be awesome, bro." There was a religious fervour in Zahid's voice.

They stopped at a wire fence. On the far side stood a domed wooden structure about twenty feet high. "It's a mosque," muttered Louise.

"Maybe one day..." The Caliph unlocked a gate and ushered them through the long grass towards a low door. They ducked inside.

As Langham's eyes adjusted to the dim green light, he tried to make sense of what he was seeing. A flat silver disc, around ten feet in diameter was situated in the centre, on a low dais. A mass of electronic equipment had been assembled on it. Langham recognised some kind of control panel and several of the cylindrical seismic sensors that kept Joanna Graham updated. They were connected to a tangle of capacitors, transformers, hard drives and circuit boards, apparently wired into a bank of lithium batteries. A black spheroid, the size of a football, hung at the centre of this web of cabling.

Langham was seized by an ancient panic. It had to be a bomb, maybe even a nuclear warhead looted from the ruins of Aldermaston...

The Caliph sensed his unease. "You believe this is some ultimate suicide mission? Think again, outside your box."

"You're building a new seismic data centre!" Joanna Graham was almost cheerful now, as if she was applauding the opening of a new upmarket health food store.

128

"This is the prototype of our new Platform. A gravitational shift device. In the years to come, we will be floating entire communities above the tortured earth. Hovering over the land as it recovers from this age of turbulence, unaffected by storms or tsunamis, we'll build a science-based Caliphate and even create an interplanetary technocracy one day—"

Langham couldn't contain his anger. "Anti-gravity propulsion is a delusion! The Nazis, the Americans, the Russians —they all fooled around with the concept for years and got nowhere. It's pseudo-science. Your people are better off digging their vegetables."

"I pity your ignorance, Doctor. But even you must know that gravity is not a force, but a change in the local geometry of space-time. And recent developments in the magneto-rotational instability of the hydromagnetic flux in the liquid core of the Earth have generated wild variations in the geomagnetic field observed on the Earth's surface and in ruptured areas of the mantle. Hence the Shift and wave after wave of seismic instability. We now know that electromagnetism and gravity influence one another enough for gravity's pull to be noticeably affected by the Earth's magnetic field. Our new superconductor technology enables us to create a spinning ball of plasma that can exploit this gravitational anomaly. And we shall rise."

Zahid raised a clenched fist. "Yo, the *shababs* will rise! I promised you a big surprise, Doc. Come on, man it was worth coming all this way!"

Louise stared at the new Platform. "Another machine. You guys always think that's the answer. That or a holy book. Anything to deny what the planet needs."

"Can you show us? Please..." Langham realised that Joanna was eager to believe anything that offered an escape from chaos.

"It is only proof of concept." The Caliph for the first time seemed defensive. "There are unresolved issues."

Langham decided to call his bluff. "I'm not expecting to be taken on a test flight. I just want to see if your gadget can rise six inches off the ground. That's all..."

"All power belongs to Allah!" Zahid''s eyes were wide with

anticipation. The Caliph nodded and embraced him before approaching the device. He paused, then murmured a prayer as he touched the control panel.

Minutes passed. Joanna was watching intently, apparently hypnotised by the lights flickering on the console. Langham peered at the rim of the disc trying to detect the slightest movement. Then he realised that the room was slowly darkening, as if its green-tinged illumination was being absorbed by the black sphere at the centre of the machine. The whole assemblage shimmered before his eyes and a throbbing low frequency wave began oscillating through his body, up through his stomach and heart into his throat and skull. Overcome with fear and nausea, he struggled to remain upright.

"It's starting to quake—get the fuck out!" Louise was shouting at him, but he could hardly walk, let alone run. Then Zahid grabbed him by the waist and dragged him towards the exit. He glimpsed Joanna, kneeling now, mesmerised by the vibrations, eyes totally focused on the dark sphere which seemed to be expanding and contracting to the same rhythm. The Caliph had prostrated himself, as if in submission to this rogue creation.

Zahid and Louise hauled him outside. They half-crawled across an expanse of turf which was slowly moving in peaks and troughs, an absurd groundswell on a convulsing planet. Langham turned in time to see the micro-platform rising briefly through the splintered wreckage of the dome before fragmenting into a hail of metal particles. Something zipped through the air. And Zahid stumbled, a red hole punctured through his forehead.

It was chilly inside the personnel carrier but Louise's torch provided a faint illumination. Outside citizens were shouting as they organised squads for sifting through debris and digging out survivors from the collapsed village hall. The quake on the golf course had also affected the High Street and rumours of the Caliph's death were causing unease. They could hear women crying.

"I must go out and help."

"They're more together than you are." It was true. Haunted by the deaths of Joanna and Zahid, he couldn't stop shivering.

"Anyway, we're here for the duration, Doctor." Another fact on the ground. The right track on the Bulldog had finally fractured, worn out by the rough terrain and Zahid's fierce driving. As the light faded they huddled for warmth, waiting for angry fists pummelling on the hatch, or the next after-shock.

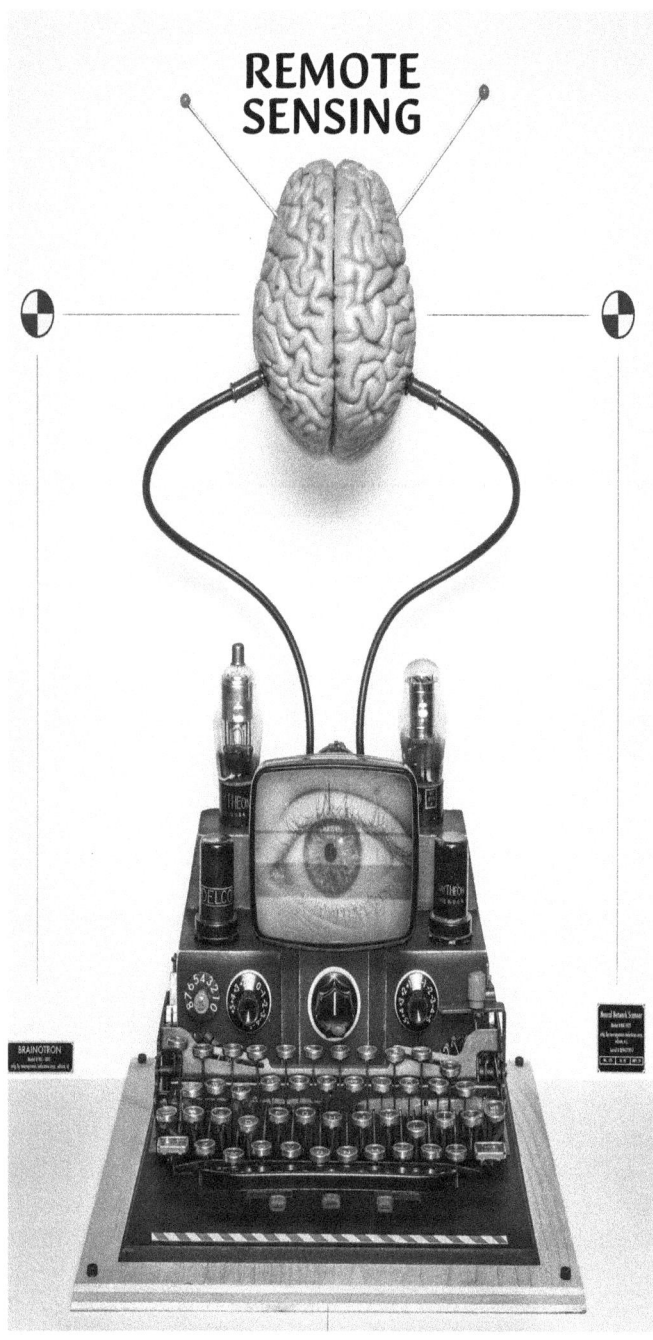

REMOTE
SENSING

LOCALE ONE

Watch Officer Colin Wright receives an emergency transmission about a suspected Meater in the village of Bovey just before dawn, almost at the end of his shift. Muzz Fielder, the neighbourhood Watch-woman operating the Retrograph, has fumbled the input as usual, allowing the needles to quiver erratically across the alphabetic display. And voltage is intermittent here. He squints in the flicker of his lantern as he tries to chalk up the name of the alleged offender on his slate, only to be left with a string of dashes and random consonants.

He curses the incompetence of this so-called 'cunning woman'. Perhaps she secretly yearns for the old-time glimmer of tiny screens. But it is his duty as Watch Officer to respond to all reports of illegal behaviour. And Bovey is little more than a hamlet. He should be able to locate the miscreant quickly and arrange appropriate sanctions. Hopefully Officer Merriweather will arrive soon to cover the day shift.

Wright yawns as he snuffs the lantern and wheels his bicycle out of the office. Bovey is only a mile away but he will be cycling against an east wind and a fine rain that will saturate his worn woollen greatcoat and obscure his glasses. He doesn't want to catch an ague again as he has every intention of making it past fifty. However, the West Shire needs rain, after the baked-earth temperatures of last summer.

He pedals up the narrow lane, avoiding pot-holes, and dodges brambles sprouting from the hedgerows. In the misty distance across the fields two bondsmen serving the Bovey Commons are harnessing an ox for the morning's ploughing. The tall one yells something, perhaps his nick-name 'Noddy', but he mustn't respond. In his position it is prudent to maintain a distance; and he's already picking up speed as the lane widens and slopes down towards the cross-roads.

He slows as he arrives at the junction. One is expected to nod the head when approaching the Memorial, positioned at the meeting point of the lane and the Bovey Road. The rusting shell of a small petroleum car, its twisted scarlet hood now bleached to a leprous pink, has been torn apart by the full-frontal impact of a corroded diesel pick-up truck—like those he's seen transporting bearded men clutching rocket launchers, in faded images of a legendary 'Middle East', that evil empire of fossil-oil. Ruptured rubber sacs spill across the crunched cabin of the hatchback. Wright sometimes wonders if the vehicles remain in their original post-collision formation or have been curated for maximum artistic effect, perhaps even imported from another accident site.

But he is always awed by the skeletal figures of the drivers and their passengers, still entangled in seat belts. Their skulls are fleshless now but the bones are still loosely draped in fluttering streamers of fabric, amid the scattered shards of fractured safety glass, now sparkling as sunlight breaks through the drifting cloudscape. The spectacle is a sharp reminder of the brutality of a world that has almost gone. Wright tells himself he should be grateful for the austere but bracing simplicities of the Greening. Even a single Meat addict threatens the stability of this new order.

As Wright cycles he can hear the faint throb of the wind-farm clustered on Hooper's Hill overlooking the village. Yet the blades on one of the turbines remain static, despite the breeze. It is rumoured that gears on the generator have seized. No one knows where to source new ones or how to fit them. There was bold talk of riding to Totting, the nearest town, to seek advice but at last month's Moot Mother Bovey over-ruled it, as a potential waste of energy. Rurals should thank Gaia for what they already had, a mantra Wright often has to repeat as he tries to intervene in neighbourly disputes over crops and boundaries. It's hard work being an Officer. But at least the rain is easing.

Muzz Fielder lives on the outskirts of Bovey in a fortified bungalow. The razor wire fencing around her sprawling allotment was erected by the previous occupant, a pharmahuasca dealer fleeing retribution from a rival urban gang-man during the Great Tumult. Fielder never bothered to remove it when she requisitioned the plot, reinforcing the ground with her own rites. She claims that the wire not only protects her in her role as Watch-woman but enhances her ability to sense the psychic currents flowing through the community. Wright doesn't believe her. He suspects she simply relies on gossip from her herbalist customers. Nevertheless, she is useful and has to be humoured.

The door is ajar. Fielder is bending over a steaming pot on her antique stove, stirring in henbane or St John's Wort or whatever she uses to create her allegedly miraculous cures. Huddled in her patchwork gown and hood, she turns and smiles awkwardly. The crusted scarifications on her broad cheeks are weeping.

'Sorry to drag you out, Officer. But there's a new Meatnik about. I feel it in my waters.'

'That's all very well, Muzz. But I can't deal with them if you don't transmit the details accurately.'

'You know me, Noddy Wright. Closer to the Earth Current than that fiddly machine. I can't always get it right first time. Let's sweeten the morning with some wine...' She shifts her acrid-smelling pottage off the stove and reaches across the table to uncork a bottle of cloudy amber liquid.

He shakes his head and unwraps his slate. 'I'd rather go through what we have so far. Now, first letter is G. So is it Grover?' Bill 'The Gasser' Grover fits the frame. Even after thirty years the former boiler technician still resents the Greening, which has eliminated his family business. And he's been recently sanctioned with the requisition of a fortnight's produce after using a cross-bow to source fox-meat.

'There's no V there, Officer Wright.' Fielder smirks triumphantly. 'Anyway, Bill's been ganged up to work on the sea wall at Torness. The coast road's flooded, it's an Aquarian thing. The stars are crafty—'

'Let's concentrate, Muzz! So that's N, not V? And still R. Come on, Muzz, you must remember.'

Fielder takes a swig from her bottle, then sighs. 'Well, it's a woman's name that's on my mind. I'll spell it out for you. G-O-N-E-R-I-L.'

'Goneril?' He's seen that name on torn pages somewhere, maybe fuelling a Solstice Pyre.

'Goneril Hawkins is the lady. She has blood on her lips, she has feasted on the animal kind!' Fielder seems to relish, perhaps even envy this transgression. Is she another secret back-slider?

But he can't be distracted. He can't be on two cases, in two places, all at once. Impossible...

'I just want to know where to find her.'

'You might find her skulking near the Tower. Now do I get my fee?'

'Later...' Wright's already through the door, desperately tired but nagged by the knowledge that he has to apprehend the offender before the Meating infection spreads.

Like most locals, Wright rarely visits the site of the Tower, formerly a Church of St Peter, according to the crooked welcoming sign. Its mediaeval stone fabric has survived the Tumult, although Pentecostalist militants—the notorious Heavy Shepherd gangs—have trashed some stained glass and Salafist jihadis from up-country tried to start a fire in the vestry.

He hurries between the overgrown graves towards the porch. The Motherhood Guild have finally given up their attempt to build a Goddess Shrine. Tangled netting intended to adorn the half-finished lump of an Earth Venus is now draped haphazardly across the tilted gravestones. 'Our art is all about decay now.' The sibilant voice intrudes from nowhere, or maybe some echoey chamber of the brain but he suppresses it. He must locate Goneril Hawkins.

He shouts her name down the nave, across the overturned pews and paces down the aisle towards the ornately carved rood screen. Then a figure emerges from behind the altar.

'So you're after me for alleged meat-crimes. That's such a tired joke...' Goneril Hawkins looks about forty, wears an old camouflage jacket, plus combat trousers with yellow boots. She's tied back her mop of dark hair with a red bandanna. Her large grey eyes glare at Wright. He stares back at her long oval face with its high cheekbones and pale skin, a different apparition from most of the Bovey womenfolk with their tanned weatherbeaten faces.

'Meat crime is hate crime. You're an offender.'

'I don't have a secret supply of sheep.'

Her crude flippancy irritates him. 'The village knows you've eaten flesh.'

'The old bag and her cronies believe I'm a cannibal, is that it?' She laughs, picks up her rucksack and turns towards the porch, but Wright lurches forward and grasps her wrist.

'Don't think you can walk away from this...' He tightens his grip and pulls her close. He smells her heavy patchouli perfume, sees that forbidden smear of crimson on her lips. 'Now if you admit your guilt nicely, I'll try and make it go easy for you at Moot, just a fast and no scourging, that's a promise.'

'Come on, Officer, you're just out for a fuck. A little frolic on the old high altar and you'll forget all about it. That's your game, but I'm not going to play it.'

Wright suppresses his anger, despite the implied slur on his professional celibacy. Sexing begot surplus children outside the hand-fasting of Mootlaw, it is 'inappropriate', a bind-word from the old codes. Her insinuation that he'd connive in her harlotry is an insult. He averts his gaze from her silver necklace, probably crafted illegally, and the intricate belt around her waist, almost certainly fabricated from deadly plastic.

'You've been salvaging cans of protein from the Ruins, I bet. Goddess knows what corruption you've brought back.' He pulls out handcuffs and clips them into place. She only grins.

'Hasn't everyone gone on a little foray over the Barrier?'

Wright has a painful back-flash of a teenage half-life, scrabbling over stone slabs and metal gantries in the fog, all bloody fingers and thumbs clawing the wire, with a vague hope of sourcing forbidden tech relics—but stumbling back empty handed at the first sweep of a search light. Thankfully the memory has morphed into a bad dream, it never really happened...

He shakes his head to stop further intrusive thoughts. The matter at hand—this belligerent woman disrespecting his rank, who doesn't appreciate the blasphemy of Meating, who sneers at him with her condescending smile. He pushes her roughly towards the nearest pillar. He must secure her there, find the nearest carter to take her directly to custody at Totting. He can't rely on her to meekly await a summons to the next village Moot. There's a tangle of old rope on the flagstones; he can guess what Shepherds used it for. He reaches for it with his free hand and fights to coil it around her waist and then pull it behind the squat stonework of the pillar, but it flops to the ground. She laughs.

'You've dreamed about this since you were a teen. Shagging the virgin on the rock. With your wrinkly face. Like a rotten apple.' She won't stop laughing while he struggles with loops and knots, breathing hard.

'Goneril Hawkins, by powers granted to me at Bovey Moot —I bind you fast for tasting flesh and blood—against Gaia's Law —you will face trial at—'

'Too late, Mister Baron Knight.' She is squirming provocatively, he is being entangled. 'It's no good, you're no good, the Dragon's coming...'

Wright senses a flash of movement at the periphery of his vision, and turns—but not fast enough to evade a sudden onslaught by barbs, darts, metallic insect-things that sting, stun, leave him delirious with pain. He is snared in wires, twitching on the ground; and a shining ovoid mask looms over him.

'I'm Regan. We're Dead Metal Girls, we rule.'

It is time to be null and void.

REMOTE SENSING

'I have seen the future and it doesn't work.' Colin Wright's optical field shimmers in prismatic colours. He is briefly aware of his wetware sampling the alt.world-lines at fifty frames a second before the vision collapses into the beige tiles of the laboratory wall.

'The manifest content of your "vision" will be analysed later,' mutters Professor Harold Godd as he removes the Zeithelm and its dreadlocks of wiring from Wright's shaven cranium. 'Bodily functions need checking first.' Wright's chest feels as if it had been punctured with red-hot needles and the sutures of his skull grind against each other as if pressurised by some sinister growth on his cortex. He wriggles in the chair like a child desperate to urinate, while Godd probes his body and tests his pulse, often glancing back at data streaming on the monitor console.

The Professor seems dissatisfied with his findings. 'I don't see any evidence that your neural microtubules actually engaged in any quantum inter-action. But then I've had serious doubts about Miss Nowak's pet theory from the start. If it wasn't for this absurd climate hysteria, she wouldn't have a budget to keep repeating these futile experiments. You can go now...'

In the cramped toilet Wright kneels and retches into the bowl. He should be grateful for his alleged gift of 'remote sensing'. By passing the Institute's battery of tests, he's won a reprieve from trying to camp out in his wrecked maisonette or sleeping on Tooting Bec Common. Admission into Dr Zofia Nowak's Remote Sensing Programme grants him a cubicle with TV, a clean mattress and regular meals, in return for his psychic surrender as a subject. But how long will the programme continue, given Professor Godd's hostility? And how long can he face the aftermath of these astral travelogues—the migraine, nausea, the whole warped ontology that forces him to grab anxiously at the toilet door handle as he positions his feet to navigate the alien perspectives of the corridor. He has to stop life-streaming...

In his room he dozes fitfully. He can't stop immersing himself in a remix of his 'Bovey' experience. The Regan-creature keeps removing her aluminium head and handing it carefully to Goneril who elevates it before the altar. 'Behold the Singularity of God,' they sing, in High Anglican voices.

He wakes up, the room buzzing into existence around him as the orderly, Suggs, prods his shoulder. 'Time for your debriefing, mate.'

Professor Harold Godd and Dr Nowak are already sitting around a table in the meeting room, listening to the cassette recording of his session. He tries to block out his reedy voice, his doppelganger's last words: 'All over, she's leaning all over me... dead metal girl... I'm null and void... get me out...'

Zofia Nowak stops the machine and flips through the typed transcript of his utterings, while the Prof fiddles with code on a laptop. Wright wants to trust the Doctor's grey eyes, her serious frown, because he likes the way she bites her lip, and that auburn pony-tail suits her and soon she will murmur in her husky Anglo-Polish accent. Her green needle-cord trouser suit is a good tight fit. It is very important to hang on to these distractions during the daily crumbling of reality. Perhaps they will offer him coffee although last time they could only manage water, because of major crop failures in Colombia or maybe tidal waves in Vietnam—there is rather a lot going on with the weather these days.

'Frankly, Colin, I am most worried.' Zofia suddenly sweeps the paperwork to one side as Godd nods in apparent agreement. 'This latest transmission seems very distorted. It won't be as bad as that, surely?'

'We're on a trajectory to the Middle Ages, if this government proceeds according to the Los Angeles Protocol. If we continue going down that time-line we're barely scratching a living from the soil, the tech's all broken, our knowledge base is disintegrating and superstition is taking over like bind-weed.'

'Isn't this some lingering climate change denialism? Despite everything that's happening? Do you really believe there could be neo-pagan religious taboos about meat consumption? Isn't this subliminal insertion triggered by your own antipathy to vegans which you've overlaid on your perceptions?'

'When you're on the street, you eat the meat...' Wright remembers lurking around upscale 'artisan' eateries at midnight, waiting to shank some foodie for his organic chicken takeaway. Those first days after his release were the hardest. From narcotics agent to predatory sub-person and then human lab rat—quantum leaps, but not the good kind.

Dr Nowak still awaits a proper answer. The curvature of the table starts to subtly distort, the hands on the wall clock tremble like the needles on that Retrograph contraption—what version of himself had tinkered with that? Was that childish nick-name really him? Colin in the Land of Nod? He seems locked into an ever-changing false memory syndrome. He breathes deeply, struggling to stabilise the vision and his voice.

'Doctor, you assured me that the Remote Sensing scenarios must depict different outcomes of our environmental policy. That's what you promised the Ministry. Enhanced guidance for crucial future-proofing. And I'm telling you what I saw, what I—ah— enacted—'

Harold Godd shuts his laptop abruptly. 'Ms Nowak, I must interject. You have just inadvertently exposed another weakness of your "quantum consciousness" theory. On your own admission this subject is acting out his unconscious biases which are simply part of a larger overarching fantasy structure— highly detailed, seemingly rich in sensory data, internally consistent, populated by apparently autonomous persons, and following a clear narrative structure. You have not created expanded quantum consciousness, whatever that is supposed to be, by resonating the lattice structure of neural microtubules. You have simply facilitated an enhanced form of lucid dreaming within the normal structures of the brain. That's an interesting epiphenomenon but that's all it is. Consciousness is merely bio-computing. You haven't liberated a time-travelling ghost in the machine. Because there isn't one.'

For a few seconds Wright feels almost relieved by the scientist's brisk dismissal of the new Bovey-reality that has enfolded him. 'He woke up and it was all a dream.' A trope he'd used himself as a kid, finishing his English homework in a hurry to get out on his new bike. Yet fussy Prof G, with his bald dome and pencil moustache, is trying to reduce him, Colin Anthony Wright, to a manageable meat puppet suspended on a few strings of code. The residual qualia of the remote vision were all too real, he can smell Fielder's foul witch-broth , sniff the Goneril woman's perfume. And what will the Doctor say? This is the most overt challenge yet to her basic premise, even to her authority as project director. She was looking down now, silently flicking through documents, maybe seeking some refutation.

Godd clears his throat. 'Ms Nowak, it's increasingly difficult for me to continue supporting this project. We might call you 'Doctor' out of courtesy and to enhance your status with your subjects but you're still not fully qualified. Obviously I've been tasked to replicate your work as part of the peer review before reporting back to the Committee and I will complete the schedule we've agreed. But your hypothesis is weak and your results are as messy as your specimens.' He glances disdainfully at Wright's grubby woollen fleece.

Wright is embarrassed, as if watching his parents about to have a row (his father stomping about ineffectually, mum mumbling bitterly). His trances and doom-dreams have formed the vortex of this current. Perhaps it would have been less stressful to have staked out the freedom of the pavements.

Nowak sighs. 'You want proof. But by the very nature of the Polyverse that's almost impossible. Every iteration of the Remote Sensing experience offers an alternate future, if only slightly. Although not all are as bleak as Mr Wright's.'

So he was Mr Wright, for once? With that formal kind of validation he could perhaps risk a question. After all, Miss Zofia isn't quite a proper doctor yet.

'Miss Nowak, how does my Remote Sensing experience compare with other subjects?' There are others, he's seen Suggs jostling them along the corridors.

'You don't want to answer that, Zofia,' murmurs Godd. 'It might compromise your data even more. Cross-contamination of fantasies, so to speak.' He allows himself a faint grin. 'I doubt if your proteges could remotely sense what is happening right here and now just ten kilometres away. In the real world.'

'Harold, the mission is to explore a range of near-future time windows to observe the likely outcomes of environmental policy. Time is against us and the Department wants a quick answer. With the limited resources we have anything else is a distraction. I already know what is now happening ten kilometres away.'

Zofia Nowak can envisage her cramped flat on the far side of London, her father in the living room, swaying in his wheelchair, probably bewildered by a din beyond the heavy shutters as another hungry mob steams down Warwick Avenue past graffitied stucco and the charred shells of BMWs. She tidies her papers and gets up. Wright realises that he isn't going to get an answer now.

'I insist on a repeatable experiment, Ms Nowak, a real-time remote viewing!' Godd taps his finger on the table, an irritated tourist demanding a room change. 'Show me that your so-called "sensitive" subjects can do what the Russians and Americans couldn't. It can't be that difficult to arrange.'

He follows her through the door and down the corridor, still needling her. Wright sits there, benumbed. So his ordeals in the Zeithelm, those time-bending hallucinations he kept crashing around in, are scientifically useless. And now there might be some new parapsychological hoop of fire that he has to leap through...

'Well, that was a quickie.' Suggs materialises in front of him. 'Off we go, then.' They march out of the room, the orderly keeping a firm grip around Wright's elbow. 'Guess you didn't have much to tell 'em—not that it's my business, you know, jobsworth and all that. But you need to keep 'em happy, even if you have to make it all up.' He opens the door of Wright's cell. 'Or else you could be out of your comfy corner, know what I mean?'

LOCALE TWO

This time the headache is worse, despite the tablets and Zofia Nowak's soft-voiced assurances while they strapped on their devices. Once again the lab begins to melt away, its geometry sagging and swaying, the walls sliding away in a dribble of his neural tissue, that's exactly what was/is happening, it will happen, they can't fool his holiness which is illuminating everything in the great bright fade to white, so this will be the famous NDE, the Near Death Experience...

I signed up for this but I'm not a significant other I'm only a signifier not a sign, a string of squiggling in the space-time, I'm a sign of the times. His voice-over chatters away in the total black/whiteness of his headspace, he is a bot in a chat-box/anti-bot in a brain-box/that is the signal his tonguing couldn't keep up with the changeling language but the sky is opening and a body is peering into him.

'I'm Regan. We're Dead Metal Girls, we rule.' Her mask gleams in the sunlight. It's smooth and blank, except for the eye-slit. Her cool tones speak directly to his inner ear. He's faintly excited by her zipped black jump suit, moulded from glossy vinyl; and wonders if he is projecting unconscious biases, as Harold Godd had insisted in a distant woozy scenario. For the Set, as the old acid psychenauts used to call it, hasn't quite settled into place, he still has sudden blinks of Godd and Nowak leaning over him, arguing about real-time remote sensing. But

143

as Regan leans closer they wobble around the edges and fade like cheap CGI.

'Dead Metal Girls—that's what the rustics call us, on our surprise appearances over there on the alt.line. But you're not in ruralist Bovey any more, we extracted you just in time. Into the right time. Into a better zoning, a new time-code. Sorry if it hurt a bit but we had to save Goneril from your repressive persona, all that half-sublimated patriarchal baggage. Just relax and recreate yourself.'

He is reclining on a couch under a manicured conifer, scanning a long sunlit lawn watered by the prismatic mist of sprinklers. In the distance, half concealed by a neat line of shrubs he can see a low-rise white building in post-modernist faux-Aztec style, crowned by a glittering dome. The skyscape is deep technicolour blue, criss-crossed with high-altitude luminous trails. The air is cool and dry.

'Here we have solutions. Come with me...' Regan supports his arm as he teeters down a neat gravelled path towards the white building. 'You're finding the transition worrying, I understand. But you will stabilise.' As they approach the glass doors, he begins walking more steadily.

'Let's relax, shall we?' They enter a high-ceilinged lounge where young women dressed similarly to Regan chat and laugh at circular silver tables, sipping from tall glasses of opaque brown liquid, their metallic face coverings tossed aside. Regan guides Wright to a table near the doors and removes her own mask.

'Go on, take a good look... Do you like what you see?' Wright's immediately drawn to her large eyes, like Goneril's but her chin and nose are more sharply defined, her lips are fuller. This could be a creature-feature of future pleasure—but the inappropriation subsides as training dictates.

A tall elderly male, clean shaven and grave-faced in a white jacket, hovers by Wright's elbow. With a discreet cough he places a tray of drinks on the table.

'Don't be alarmed. Hermes is a fully trained synth and understands the value of service.' Regan raises a glass. 'Here's to us!'

144

The liquid tastes sour but he controls the gagging reflex. 'It's good for the anterior singular cortex,' Regan assures him. 'It will reduce your negative self-focus.'

He hears himself ask what is happening, as if his voice is operating via remote control. It is all very awkward, like a replay of some semi-exhumed teen doltishness with a smart bird from Chelsea.

'It will be easier, Colin, when we have been to the Opera. All will be explained through art. That's the best way. Now drink up!'

He gulps down the oily fluid and follows her through an archway into a steeply raked auditorium. The seating is arranged around a projecting stage. 'We'll go right to the front. They won't bite.' People smile and make room for them as they find their seats.

The lights dim. A spotlight picks out the head and shoulders of a woman, dark hair severely cut and bobbed, standing erect in a broad-shouldered business blazer. Her eyes close, her pointed jaw quivers and her lips begin to move as she projects a high soprano note, a controlled scream. 'It is a song of power,' whispers Regan. 'A pure F sharp. And just listen to the processing on that voice!' The scream rises by microtones, an ultrasonic ghost tone drilling into Wright's skull.

Then small dark figures rush about in strobe-light, a choreography of fractured stop motion, abrupt transitions and freezes, a broken dance that keeps re-creating itself in new angular postures. The soprano scream soars over a deep thudding heartbeat, driving the dancers in their metallic masks through their manic intersections, flashing in and out of being/not-being visible. 'Ah, the quantum jerk! Every particle doing its bit...' Regan is ecstatic. 'The Dead Metal will live. Our Inner Elves are directing us. You will see...' Wright's hearing is overloaded and the rhythm pulses up his spinal column. A voice chants over thrash guitars and drums. It is his own.

FANTASY ROBOTS
SEXUALLY VIABLE!
FANTASY ROBOTS

VERY RELIABLE!
I CAN'T TRUST
MY BIONIC LUST
IT LEAVES ME IN A STATE OF DISTRACTION
 IMAGINE SCENES
WITH THESE LOVING MACHINES
I CAN'T CONTROL A STRANGE ATTRACTION

The woman in the suit is conducting his punk oratorio with sweeping gestures. He's on a loop, he can't stop even though his throat is raw with the shout, a shout out of the dark.

Then everything stops, including the woman's high-frequency squeal. She utters, with cold deliberation:

I will lick you with my qualia
you'll like how I fake it

so love my qubits
taste and test
my sweet bytes

I will like you

carbon fool

'How about that? Kleo, our first great trans-human poet!' Regan grips Wright's hand in her excitement, but his stomach is curdling with dread, he doubles up in his seat, trying not to vomit. The smart people along the row pretend not to look but the woman in the suit stares at him accusingly.

'I think it's time to get you home.' Regan levers him out of his seat and pushes him up the aisle.

Soon he is in a bed somewhere. Regan is leaning across him, he can see her ghostly breast in the blue gloom and she's easing him in, which is sweet but quite cold, like her finger tips. As she fucks him, she whispers about the successful terraforming of the planet and the redemption of its biodiversity. 'Our secret's in our solar satellites... cloud control... nano-crystal cells...

and these tidal platforms... back and forth... back and forth... flowing nicely... all that energy... good energy... so good... trying so hard...very hard... working on all our senses... so hard... going beyond....' Her voice breaks off in a faint moan. She is a naughty knowbot or a notnik, he can't know yet, the icy gnosis goes rippling and ripping through him, he trips as he travels into a burst of light...

RAPID TRANSIT

Zofia's journey home is disrupted at Oxford Circus by 'a person under a train' at Regent's Park. That's the official version— although she suspects there's been flooding again. As staff herd grumbling commuters along the platform, she decides to take the escalator to Oxford Street and walk to Tottenham Court Road station where she can pick up an alternative route back via the Northern Line. If she's lucky she might get a seat and the chance to study a transcript of the latest Colin Wright session.

But the Oxford Street exit is jammed with shouty people brandishing banners and placards—and as the crush sweeps her on to the paveme0nt she realises too late that she's going to be caught up in a typical Friday afternoon protest. She can only move along with the relentless surge of the crowd. Crushed on one side by a bald topless man with a tattooed beer belly—It's My Body and I'll Die if I Want To—she lurches into the body space of a spindly woman waving a hand scrawled cardboard sheet—The New Food Burns!—who grins eagerly as if spotting a fellow-conspirator and yells something. But her syllables are drowned in the roaring torrent of noise—samba drumming, whoops and whistles, distorted megaphonics proclaiming diverse and conflicting freedoms. Zofia is almost choked by the swirling pink and orange smoke of flares and struggles to maintain her balance. Some yards ahead of her a Ronald McDonald clown on stilts sways uneasily. To stumble here would risk death by stampede. Day-glo placards bobs up and down over the throng. —HUNGER IS ANGER!— FIGHT THE MEAT TAX! Police lines are forced back on to the pavement, unable to kettle the swelling mob. People hurl bunches of flowers, doggybags of shit.

Then a small object is thrown from a third floor window high over a budget fashion store further down the street. A cheer goes up even as it falls, to land about twenty metres ahead of her, amid the forest of signs demanding legalised pharmahuasca.

A fireball, a glitter of smashed glass, a micro-tornado of dirty smoke, a brief deafness before the screams.

The fat man moans, clutching his shoulder. Marchers hit the ground, a few jump up for a better view, and people retreating trip over those pushing forward. Zofia is trapped, numb with fright, there's nowhere to go.

Someone lobs a second grenade from an adjacent window. The spindly woman tries to shield her head with her banner while Zofia crouches and covers her face. The blast is louder this time.

She risks looking up and glimpses a hooded figure kneeling on the roof with a machine gun. 'Duck and cover! Duck and cover!' A blonde woman, I-Heart-Texas on her T-shirt, screams in her ear, rolling herself into a foetal ball to hide from the deafening rattle of bullets but one gets her in the chest. Blood clots the Lone Star State.

Zofia crawls towards the entrance of a cafe, elbowing her way through bodies, between the scrum of boots and entangled legs, expecting to die at any moment. The doorway has been boarded up in expectation of rioters but the chipboard is broken and she manages to push it back with a thrust from her bruised shoulder. She staggers to the far end of the room and collapses behind the counter.

Outside across the street a policeman with a pistol is peering up from behind an overturned van and returning fire, filmed by a citizen journalist who is hit in the forehead as he turns for a nice shot of the sniper. Then a figure leaps from the roof, shouting incoherently. But his backpack explodes prematurely in mid air, leaving fragments of flesh and droplets of blood to rain down on the crowd below.

A black banner is unfurled from the third floor window:
NO LIVES MATTER

FAST FORWARD

Zofia Nowak won't listen to her father.

'Please, Zofia. You must not go to Institute today. Too dangerous now on subway.'

'I'll be OK, *Tato*. So will you. Melanie from the agency is coming in as usual. She'll tidy up and do you a nice lunch, soup and dumplings.'

'Soup is nothing. It is you, *Malenka*! You can't stop shaking, even now. I see TV news. All channels. You are lucky to be alive.'

'The work's very important. We need to act fast. If we're going to find a way forward.'

'What way? You put wires around brains of criminals and they tell you bad dreams. What kind of science is that? Anyway, you can do work from home.' He swivels his chair towards his desk in the corner alcove. 'Look, use my computer. I will be quiet as my graveyard and read my new magazine.'

It has been a mistake, even a serious breach of security, to have given him even a hint of what went on at that nondescript office block in Lambeth. But isolated in the apartment his appetite for information is his primary drive.

She tries to concentrate on checking her handbag as he returns to his old obsession. 'I'm no fool, Zofia. I know true science. Rocket science!' It is indeed the truth. If history had subdivided differently Stanislaus Nowak, top-flight engineering student from the University of Krakow, might have migrated eastwards to Krasnoyarsk and worked on Vostok and Soyuz but when the pious men with the big moustaches took over, Soviet sympathisers had nowhere to go but out. As he huffs and settles back in his wheelchair, trying to hide his hurt and anxiety behind his copy of *New Scientist*, Zofia struggles with her love and exasperation. After *Mamusia* died, in the M5 collision with a pick-up truck that left him half-paralysed, he'd set his roughcast features into a stoic mask, as brutalist as his haircut, while urgently needing to enclose his daughter in a protective zone.

'*Tato*, I promise I'll be safe.'

'Are any of us safe? With bombs in city centre? And troubles, even here.'

'The local security people will be around. And you have my number, too.'

'Security? Say what you will about General Jaruzelski, under him children were not burning cars for their fun.'

'All quiet now. And the main door will be double locked. See you later. I must go now.' She kisses his forehead.

There are no fresh atrocities this morning on her brisk walk to the Tube, or on the crowded Bakerloo train that races non-stop through Oxford Circus, or during her sprint to the Institute. She ignores the newsfeed on her phone and manages to keep her mind clear, in the moment. But according to her wristband nitrous oxide concentration in Lambeth is 137 micrograms per cubic metre. Mobility is hard work. She should have read the new Colin Wright material last night, but after nearly a bottle of Merlot to help her sleep...

Suggs barely glances at her ID as she negotiates the turnstile and hurries towards her office. She expects him to ask her about Oxford Street—he knows she commutes through the West End—but his eyes are downcast. It's as if he's sensed her potential victimhood and is afraid of being somehow infected by her proximity to the horror.

Harold Godd is sitting behind her desk looking smug. 'Update! I've taken the initiative in debriefing Wright.'

'Without me? That's against our agreement!'

'I could play you the tape but there's really little point. He now claims he was apported to some techno-utopia at least thirty years in the future, where our climate was controlled by advanced technology and entertainment was provided by people dressed up as robots or robots bio-formed as people—he wasn't quite sure which. But there was more of this preoccupation with sex, he actually had some kind of coition with his guide, this Regan construction. It's all very inappropriate—and so obviously an old adolescent fantasy.'

'But he envisioned a scenario where high-tech climate control really worked? Carbon capture perhaps? Maybe we have good news for the Ministry.'

'Another fantasy! Like his soft pliable female robotics. Do you want to confuse our policy makers with his delusions?

Just abandon your emotional attachment to this dream of quantum paranormal hi-jinks in the microtubules of neurons. Unless you can repeatedly demonstrate remote sensing in our ordinary boring everyday space-time continuum. It should be simple enough to set it up. I'm off now to a meeting of the sub-committee. When shall I tell them to expect a re-design of the experiment?'

He pats her elbow as he left. She recognises it as a control tactic he'd probably learned from a Power Point on his recent academic management training module. She is trembling again, trying to fade out a replay of her Oxford Street ordeal. She couldn't tell Godd she was there. He'd only try to use it in some way, to prise open her vulnerabilities.

For the first time she experiences a spasm of doubt about her working hypothesis. Perhaps her technique of transcranial ultrasonic stimulation is only an elaborate way of inducing enhanced dreaming. There is no proof that any of her subjects have developed focused precognition or any other form of ESP. Colin Wright's latest sessions are the most sustained and coherent narratives so far but they contradict each other and include so many bizarre details. The remote sensing talent is roguish, unpredictable, an agent of chaos. How could Wright's gift (or curse) be anchored in the present? She has to risk crossing the boundary between researcher and subject.

She discovers Wright in the residential day room, where a bored Suggs lounges by the door minding Mrs Ponsford, a self-identifying 'sensitive' from Torquay, and the old Dubliner Patrick Kiff, who rambles on about 'second sight in the Celtic twilight.' They sit apart on the worn leatherette sofa, their rapid-eye movements following *The Great Fat British Celebrity F**k-Up*, rising in the ratings on daytime TV. Mrs Ponsford clucks her disapproval at a quick zoom of an obese man clenching a sizzling flare between his buttock cheeks but Mr Kiff is praying for another glimpse of the hyperactive presenter, a blonde in a thong.

Wright is standing by the barred window, looking five storeys down at a convoy of military trucks crawling through rain and the morning commuter jam. She pulls up chairs and beckons to him. They exchange a formal good morning. She can't help noticing his stubbly chin and egg stains on his dark blue fleece. His glasses are flecked with dandruff.

'We shouldn't give up, Colin. It's important to keep your self respect. I know it's hard.'

He suspects a stratagem. Why this charm offensive and sudden concern for his welfare?

'Sorry you're not getting the data you need. But it's out of my control, you understand.'

'That's exactly what I want to ask you. About control...'

'Well, you should know, Doctor Nowak. You're the ones in control. You and Godd.'

'Colin, remember that the program is voluntary. You can leave at any time.' Freedom, that old clickbait. To jerk him back to the street, the stench of shelters. Or old contacts with unfinished business plans...

'So what do you want to know? I babble everything out during the sessions, I hack myself right open, all kinds of intimate stuff, every last detail. You did the pre-session hypno-briefings, gave me the target dates. You've got my body stats, everything.'

'And I'm very grateful for your co-operation, your skill in articulating everything. But I'm taking about time-control.'

'Time. Time after time in the Time-Hat. I put it on and on it goes. Nothing I can do about that.'

'We've been operating on the basis that each projection

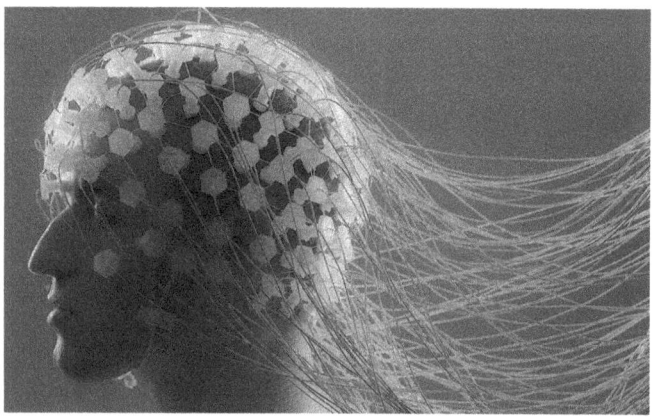

152

session takes the subject forward in time, is a form of internalised time acceleration to a specific target and dateline.'

'You've been operating... That's great... But I'm the operative! I don't have any choice. You wouldn't understand unless you went through with it yourself... once the process starts it's unstoppable... a sense of pressure... always rising onwards and upwards... through the white-out to dateline twenty-fifty... or whatever decade it's supposed to be. Look, I don't fucking know any more!' He's shouting now, Mrs Ponsford is looking uneasy and Suggs is on his way over, handcuffs swinging from his belt.

'You OK there, Doc? Is our Colin falling out of his pram?'

'It's all right, Mr Suggs. He's just stressed.' Zofia takes Wright's hand. 'Colin, we're going to simplify the time issues, make some adjustments. We're going to keep you in the present tense. And set up some simple tests. Then everything will be much more straightforward.'

'This is Godd's idea, isn't it?'

'We need a verifiable experiment if they're going to renew the funding. Then we can try more future remote sensing, more opportunities for you to use your unique talent, enjoy new adventures in the continuum. Otherwise...'

Otherwise science will let him go. Another expulsion into outer darkness. To a city of dread night, spiked doorways, locked toilets. Grit, fumes and rain. Moving right along, nowhere to sit. Or bagged up on a bench, a quaint detail for top-knotted psycho-geographers to log on their daily rounds. Or manacled to a chair facing old acquaintances. Or even returning to the maisonette—his terminal trauma zone. No, not there. He has to pass the test.

'So I've got to jump through Godd's hoops. His circus, but I'm your monkey...'

'I promise you my full support. I know what you've been through to get here.'

Wright scowls. She doesn't know half the story.

OVERVIEW

Midnight at the Institute, all quiet in the lab. Wright must submit

153

to the new experimental procedure, he has no choice. This is his destiny. 'Mektoub—it is written.' The dry laconic wheeze of an old American writer, remote, like fluttering tape echo...

Two muscular male nurses settle him in the chair, crown him with the Zeithelm. He is enthroned. Didn't the Americans once have an electric chair in Philadelphia for establishing telepathic contact with battleships? Some top secret that his former line manager, an old conspiracy enthusiast, had imparted in his narco days? No matter, at least we Brits had finally equalled the Americans at something, our remote sensing was a thing. At least he was a thing, the object of the operation.

Zofia appears. Tonight she has spiked up her hair, revealing her high forehead, highlighting her resemblance to a TV actress he liked as a child, a kind of spaceship-mistress. New uniform too: grey tunic and trousers, purple scarf. She's attempting a reassuring smile as she hands him a thick white envelope, sealed and taped.

'Let's go through it once more. In here are the geographic coordinates of the target location. I have not seen them, I don't know the place they refer to. The only person who does is Dr Harold Godd, who selected them using the output of a random number generator.'

Wright looks around, carefully so as not to dislodge the cables of the helmet. The male nurses are re-setting the ultrasound equipment to new parameters, as instructed by Doctor Nowak. Beyond them, by the door, Mr Suggs stands guard over Mrs Ponsford and Mr Kiff, sitting expectantly in their dressing gowns, as if for a late-night silver screening.

'The Professor is currently away from the Institute for the duration of the session. As the ultrasonics start, you will, as agreed, attempt to divine the coordinates written in this envelope and bi-locate to them. When you return from your altered state you will draw, from memory, the scene you have witnessed. Then our witnesses will compare your drawing with an image of the target location.'

He stares at the envelope and turns it over and over. Is he supposed to pierce the paper with psychic laser-vision and blind-read the digits of the co-ordinates? He can't even read an

154

ordnance survey map, let alone relate its latitudes and longitudes to a hot spot on the surface of the Earth.

'We'll begin when you're ready.' He'll never be ready, he is a victim of his self-imposed imposter syndrome. But onwards and inwards. He nods.

The nurses slide on the rubber sleeve to measure his blood pressure and tighten the chest belt that monitors respiration. As they run a final check on the connections to the transducers in the Zeithelm he's suddenly anxious for his bodily safety, for the first time. 'An experiment is also a risk'. Who said that? Professor Bernard Quatermass, no less. But that was ghostly black and white TV, rockets and monsters. When Wright first joined the programme, charming Doctor Zofia assured him that adverse effects were very rare. At high stimulation intensity, the process might cause haemorrhage, cell death or damage, and unintentional blood-brain barrier opening. But that was after intense stimulation above safety limits. They won't scramble his deep brain, surely. He's an asset, isn't he?

Lights blink on a monitor. Yet this time the induction process is different. No headlong rush, that vertiginous sense of free fall into the timescape. The transducers press on his scalp and the walls of the laboratory sit firmly around him. He seems grounded by a kind of sleep paralysis, he can't even move a finger.

Then his torso jerks and his point of view alters, as if he's a camera rising in a slow but steady crane shot. Yet glancing down he can see a clone of himself still strapped in the entanglement of his headgear, hands gripping the arms of the chair. There's the sense of a high frequency hum, just beyond the limits of his hearing—and a queasy sensation spiralling around his solar plexus. Something alien is extruding from his navel, a silver umbilical is uncoiling as he rises towards the fluorescent strip lighting on the ceiling. It keeps snaking out, out of his control...

His senses are tricking him. This is a misinterpretation of the laboratory cabling; or maybe cultural conditioning, a misremembering of some crumpled paperback on astral travel that an old hippy in a shed had thrust upon him. But his astral body instinctively knows what to do. He has previous form, after all. He keeps rising, the silver tentacle from his solar plexus spirals down like a strand of spectral superglue, thinning to a fine thread as he ascends, Christ-like, through foggy layers of concrete and roof asphalt, into the night sky.

And he's droning over the lights of South London, its terraces, tower blocks, multi-storey carparks, a museum, kebab shops, re-purposed churches, a gym, all turning and turning beneath him in a flaring orange halo as he tries to orient himself, in panic mode. He can't think in a straight line but that's the only way to navigate, you have to think it through and it will happen. And then he realises that his course has already been set, he's stabilising around a beam, a signal responding to whatever data was enclosed in the envelope. It's an amazing trick. He can identify as a flying object. He's in the right body. He's going to be on the case, on target.

There's a luminous miasma over the city like a blend of carbon, chemical and electromagnetic emissions, a radiant smog. It seems to cluster around the densely populated residential areas, over mansard roofs or around the bay-windows of extended semis. The vapour drifts out from the balconies of high rises, between clusters of satellite dishes and phone masts, across the car parks of all-night superstores, through dank subways and under-passes.

He fights against the realisation but he can't escape the recognition. This mist is an astral phenomenon, an auric pollution, the ghostly effluent of humanoid presence, old Madam Blavatski's subtle body odours, thought-forms adrift on the night wind, the discharge of dreams. And maybe he's just an eddy in the current. If his psychic landline broke and his connection was torn away, he'd dissolve, swirl off into dark matter—

If you think it, it will happen. Magical thinking is the first stage of self destruction here. If he is going to stay in orbit he must resist the phantasms, these fantasy robotics that replay old mind-games and horror shows. He is in an altered state of consciousness, but this is surely a controlled experiment. He will drive his psyche and pass the test, he will survive it.

London is speeding up beneath him. He overflies the

various tourist sites, the mausoleums of state, the palaces and Parliament. Anyone would think he was on a suicide mission. He ducks and dives around the winking lights of a police helicopter tracking a suspect vehicle over the Chiswick flyover, only to find himself instantly over the Regent's Park Mosque, and then locking on to the faint psycho-emanations of Zoo creatures, the dreams of cheetahs and snakes in their darkened pseudo-jungles.

Then it's one jump cut after another, he vaults over the rooftops, in and out of attic windows, through brick, plaster, wood, lead, all those barricades of dead matter. He's wide-eyed, the flying I. He's going in, there's a window of opportunity, he's ON TARGET, he's about to crash into—

STATE OF THE ART

Wright has blank page syndrome. An immaculate sheet of cartridge paper has been spread across the table. They've laid out a rainbow array of pens, pencils and pastels. And they've left him alone in this windowless sealed room, with a recorder running to capture any commentary on the process of recording his remote night flight.

The issue is not too little but too much. 'Too much information in the target zone,' he mutters. 'It's surreal—sorry, overworked word. It was real but very remote. It was somehow so—sensual.' His tone is elegiac. But he tells himself this isn't art work, it is only documentation.

He chooses a fine black pen and outlines an enclosed space, a room viewed through the fourth wall. A smallish bedroom. He's adding a window, with locked wooden shutters. Colour the walls a pale green. He sketches a dead light bulb and hints at inverted pyramids of illumination from the uplighters. Here's a rumpled bed, striped quilt, blue ceramic lamp with orange shade on the bedside table. On the floor, a pile of notebooks and tatty folders. He's speeding across the page now, deploying colour and line with total control. This won't be the usual scribble and daub you see with remote viewers, he's going hyper-realist with his shading and cross hatching.

He should have gone to art school. There's a black bra and panties scattered across the pillows, a saucy touch, you don't get that with Uri Geller. He's adding a low bookshelf under the window. He can't fit the titles on the spines but thinks he can remember—*The Blizzard* by Vladimir Sorokin; *Varieties of Religious Experience* by William James; *Consciousness Explained* by Daniel Dennett; *Solaris* by Stanislaus Lem; *The Emperor's New Mind* by Roger Penrose and even Saul Wolfe's *Love Slaves of the Forest Queen*, which seems louche but he saw what he saw. On the far wall a worn poster for Neutron Spyder, always big in Eastern Europe. And a cheap reproduction print of Rousseau's *The Dream*, depicting the painter's Polish mistress reclining naked on a couch in a jungle landscape crowded with exotic plants and animals. Over the bed, faded family photos, perhaps—a young mother sitting proudly in a red VW Beetle, baby girl on the safety seat beside her. On a chest of drawers—a jar of cold cream, eyeliner, a candle in an empty vodka bottle and a trumpet, somewhat tarnished. The intricacies of the detail and his total recall are wondrous.

It's a masterpiece, worth the vertigo and queasiness he still feels several hours after they removed him from the chair and escorted him to this controlled area.

'I've drawn everything I can remember. I was there. And that's that.' He presses a buzzer. Any moment now they'll be in there to seal up his vision and stick him back in his cubicle. Now everything depends on Harold Godd's private view.

VOYEURINGS

Professor Harold Godd doesn't want any surprises. Although the experimental protocols aren't as tight as he would have liked, the team need to resolve matters quickly. The outcome from this afternoon's session will drive a giant stake through the heart of this remote sensing fantasy once and for all, as far as the scientific community is concerned. In any case Wright has been dubious from the outset, an unreliable subject with a criminal past, who made some very odd admissions while surfacing from his allegedly trans-temporal trance states. It might be best if the cassette documenting his 'techno-future' trip was 'lost' or at least withheld.

As Suggs spreads black plastic portfolios over the meeting room table Godd recalls some of his most reliable results, all documented in peer-reviewed articles. No wonder the tabloids call him *The Paranormal Terminator.* He has exposed so many frauds: that metal bender on breakfast TV with his pre-stressed spoons; bogus precogs who'd marked up their Zener cards; and famous medium Terry Taverna, cold-reading the bereaved in Wimbledon Theatre, helped by his glamorous assistant Marlene who'd checked them out on Facebook in advance. As for remote sensing, people will project what they want to see in those random scrawls when they compare them to the target. It has been a perfect storm across the generations: the ADHD attention span deficit accelerated by social media; the direct effects of electromagnetism on the brain among the aged; the use of psychotropic drugs among the young. All the subjects Nowak has tested on her program are infected by apophenia, they see connections multiplying everywhere. Her star protege Colin Wright is the worst of all. However, the man's claims will soon be discredited.

Enter reserve test subjects, Mrs Beryl Ponsford and Mr Patrick Kiff, overawed by the privilege of entering this administrative sanctum. They sit, as directed by Suggs, glancing uneasily around the room. Zofia Nowak hurries in, eager to reassure them.

'As I explained, all you have to do is look very carefully at the four pictures we are going to show you. One of them is an image of the actual target location. It could be a photo, it could be a drawing. We want you to be witnesses as you compare them and select the one you think is the most likely target. Is that all good?'

'I will know anyway, before your Professor's target place is revealed.' Mrs Ponsford, flaunting her new blue-rinse perm, is quietly confident. 'Silver Fox and his spirit workers will guide me on the Astral...'

'And I know the ways of the Fey Folk, their wits are quick to reveal tricksters!' Mr Kiff will not be upstaged. Godd is intrigued, almost impressed by the depth of their convictions. These people use their belief systems like Zimmer frames. Despite all the obstacles they just keep going.

Across the table there's a video camera on a tripod, for documentation. Zofia switches it on. It's time for him to leave the room for the duration of the viewing. He can't risk his body language giving the subjects a subliminal cue. But he'll be back...

'Right, we can begin.' She nods to Suggs. Wearily, like an adult participating in a children's party game, the orderly unzips a portfolio and empties it.

'Oh, that's quaint. You know, I swear I walked down that street when Ponsford was courting me. It's one of those little villages—the name will come to me.' Mrs Ponsford studies a picture postcard. It depicts a view down a narrow street, nineteenth century frontages rendered in cream and pale blue, sash windows flanked by neo-classical pilasters. The nearest building is perhaps some kind of social club, which displays a banner over its doorway, but because of the angle of the shot, it can't be deciphered.

'It's Masonic, you can be certain of that,' Mr Kiff wags a finger of warning. 'They'll be in there, wearing their Satanic regalia, plotting against church and state. They'll have us for target practice, to be sure!' Beryl Ponsford purses her lips. The name of the location refuses to come, but it's on the tip of her tongue. Memory is such a blur...

'We need to focus our attention on what's actually in the image, Mr Kiff. That's essential!' Zofia fears the subjects will start dissipating their attention in squabbles. She should never have taken crusty old Kiff on board. But he'd done well on the initial psychometry test, identifying that wrist watch as owned by a former security guard, the poor guy stabbed in the attack on that synth-food laboratory in Bristol. Maybe acts of violence did leave their mark on the aetheric field, whatever that was. Oxford Street and the blood of the bursting man have left their psychic stigmata on her. But she has to keep numb and carry on. 'Next one, please, Mr Suggs.'

'This doesn't look very spiritual,' declares Mrs Ponsford. They're looking at a large colour photo, an overhead shot, probably from a low-flying drone, showing some sort of light industry park. It's overcast. Rows of cars are lined up outside a long building, two storeys, modern breeze block construction with grey weatherboarding, a low pitched roof with skylights. It's bordered by shrubbery and high fencing. Two figures have been captured walking out of the only exit. It's hard to distinguish too much detail from this viewpoint but one, a male might be wearing overalls. He's holding the elbow of a female, long blonde hair, in a kind of silver plastic trouser suit. Perhaps he's escorting her to one of the vehicles on the tarmac.

Mr Kiff is not impressed by the silver trousers. 'Those fashions are a grave scandal. There's far too much immorality these days. And on that television, God help us! Like seductions by the wicked elves and fairy folk. Now I can tell you, Mrs Ponsford, as a matter of actual fact , that I have— '

'That's quite enough, Mr Kiff. We need to keep calm.' The tired British T-shirt mantra. Zofia needs that bromide. The experiment could slip out of her control. She wonders what Colin Wright has drawn—the picturesque village street, the business park? Odd that Godd's supposedly random co-ordinates have so far both thrown up scenes that are recognisably somewhere in the UK.

Suggs zips open the third envelope and a picture flutters to the surface of the table. It's another photo, faded black and white, newsprint quality. An arid landscape, desert scrub, empty skies. In the middle distance there's a tangle of wreckage near a concrete block house, its walls scorched and cracked, its roof collapsed.

No-one speaks for a moment. 'I feel a cloud of terrible evil. Terrible... ' Mrs Ponsford has gone grey faced, sitting stiff in her cardigan and sensible shoes like an old mannequin. 'Can you turn it over, please?' Mr Kiff's eyes are closed. He breathes, heavily.

Zofia has known this image since her student activist days, marching with her trumpet in the Campaign for Nuclear Disarmament, now disbanded. She recognises the remains of Survival City, that 'Doom-Town' built in the Nevada desert in the 1950s to test the destructive power of nuclear bombs, a mile from ground zero but close enough for the dummies to melt. She's certain this is the image that has materialised from Godd's mystery co-ordinates. It makes intuitive sense that his covert urge to destroy, to reduce all hope, would through sheer synchronicity intersect with this target. And this surely is the dead landscape that awaits them all if they can't control the superheated planet.

'I think we've seen enough. Let's move on.' So the fourth image must be Colin's drawing. Which one of the three will it resemble? She's certain it will be a sketch, however crude, of that bomb site. Zofia steps back to check the camera while Suggs lays the picture in front of them and turns it over. They pore over it, blocking her view.

'Now that's what I call a picture. Neat drawing and nice colouring-in. Don't you agree, Patrick? I think this could be the one.' Mrs Ponsford sounds relieved, even Mr Kiff has perked up.

'Well, maybe not for the National Gallery. But you know what everything's meant to be, none of your Picasso fol-de-rol. It looks real enough. Mind you, I'm not sure about the painting on the wall and that bed's a terrible mess. If this is a lady's bedroom, then I must say that she's no better than she should be, if you get my drift. I wonder what the Doctor thinks.'

Doctor Zofia looks—and is silent. Silenced. A chilly panic. A cognitive rupture. She must not believe what she's seeing. An impossible vision, the baddest dream. Somehow—how?—her private zone, her sanctuary has been laid bare. Her space has been violated. She's been exposed, stripped, outed as a slut-face. Her room with its modest treasures. Her empty muddled bed. Even her grubby underwear.

Wild thoughts. Her father must have blundered in, taken a photo, mailed it to Colin Wright, to sabotage the credibility of her experiment, which he thinks is ridiculous because it's not fucking rockets. That must be it. But it can't be, her tata loves her, doesn't he? She's trembling again.

'I'm getting a definite vibration,' whispers Mrs Ponsford. 'I'm certain this is that stupid professor's target. It's funny when it happens—like you're walking through the fog, a real pea-souper—and then Silver Fox's spirit helpers touch your hand and take you to this lovely room. What did you think, Patrick?'

'I wouldn't call it lovely, Mrs P. I have a bad feeling this is the place. A fairy trap indeed.'

162

Zofia mechanically hands them forms and pencils. Her voice seems remote, uttered through her, not by her. 'If you could be so kind... Just confirm your choice in writing and add any other comments you have.'

'Don't worry, dear. I think we've said everything. I like to think that we've been helpful. Some people don't take us seriously, you know, but you're quite different. ' Mrs Ponsford ticks a box and hands back the paper with a smile. Mr Kiff takes his time but eventually makes his mark. He starts writing something but crosses out his scribble and stares at the sheet.

'Make your mind up, Mr K. I'm sure Mrs Ponsford would like a cup of tea in the common room, with a nice bun, after all this—wouldn't you, Beryl?' Suggs cajoles, almost flirtatious, in holiday camp redcoat mode. He snatches Kiff's form.

For Zofia, the banter might as well be in an alien tongue. As Suggs escorts her subjects out, she gazes blankly at Wright's drawing of her sanctuary.

She can hear voices in the corridor. Godd and an unfamiliar female voice, curt and emphatic. Heels clicking on the parquet.

The Professor enters, accompanied by a tall dark haired woman, severe of face, about forty, in a charcoal business suit with ruched shoulders, striding briskly in her long skirt. She's holding a large white envelope and a black laptop case.

'Zofia, this is Thea Dunwell. She's our Verifier. She will—.'

Dr Nowak isn't interest in courtesies. Her terror has morphed into rage.

'You set this up, Harold! You got some intelligence goon to take pictures of my bedroom or you planted some camera bug and got someone to sketch the photo. Maybe you put pressure on my poor old father to collaborate. I don't know. You chose me as your target. Don't deny it!'

'Surely you would be pleased if your star pupil gave you a definitive proof of remote viewing. But what makes you think he succeeded? I suppose you believe that there is some kind of telepathic link between you. Let's see what Ms Dunwell will tell us. And make sure that camera is still running.'

Dunwell runs her pearl finger nail along the seam of the envelope. A slip of yellow paper falls out.

'Now Doctor, please read the coordinates for me.' The digits dance in front of Zofia's eyes but she manages to hold the paper steady. Robotically she reads off latitude and longitude in degrees. Thea Dunwell boots up a Google map and inserts the details. She selects the aerial view option on the display which spins through blue, green and brown as she scales down the image—to low altitude surveillance of a business park. Cars are lined up outside a low- rise modern industrial building with grey cladding and skylights. Small figures are captured walking across the tarmac.

Zofia doesn't understand. This image is so banal. It could be a JPEG for a corporate website. This is the least likely target site of all the four pics. An apocalyptic wasteland would somehow make sense.

'Sorry it's not your cosy domestic interior. But that site is the target as identified by the numbers, which were of course generated at random. It's obvious that Wright couldn't read them through his supposed talents for psychometry and bi-location. He has just drawn an elaborate fantasy, based on his knowledge of you.'

'That's ridiculous. He doesn't know me. He has never visited my home, let alone my bedroom.'

'His pretty picture is a projection—you've obviously dropped clues about your tastes. Perhaps he has hacked into pictures on your phone. Dare I suggest that you might also have private images, even bedroom scenes, out there in the cyber sphere? Sexting, I believe it's called.'

Zofia can't believe what she is hearing. But Godd has the emotional intelligence of a robot. He keeps grinding away, he is determined to discredit her on every level.

'Such mundane details have probably influenced him. But the key point is that his remote vision is wildly off-target. It's nonsensical.'

Zofia can't believe his sexism and obtuseness. How he will relish detailing her humiliation when he reports back to the subcommittee. It could be the end of any serious attempt to investigate remote sensing—and the termination of her research career. Already Dunwell, eyes down and poker faced,

164

is clicking away on her computer, compiling her verification of this embarrassment.

'We must try again. Surely you want a repeatable experiment. J.B. Rhine at Duke University did hundreds, even thousands of operations—'

'—that only proved his bias and confirmed his wishful thinking. And you don't have time. None of us have time. Even you must realise this project was frivolous. It was a bizarre idea from the start, worthy of the last days of Hitler. If you hadn't fooled an incompetent university administration, you would never have had the funding in the first place. And the blundering Civil Service idiocrats were clutching at straws, desperate not to get it wrong, hoping to find a positive outcome of our wretched Los Angeles Protocol pledges. Perhaps they were looking for reassurances that everything was going to turn out nicely. Thankfully they've got an expert like myself on-board to prevent any more time and money being wasted.'

He turns to Ms. Dunwell. 'You see, Thea, what I have been up against! Institutionalised pseudo science, a mash of neurological fakery and bogus "quantum" pataphysics, all stirred up with a big spoonful of New Age psychobabble.'

Zofia looks Dunwell in the eye, that glassy eye. 'Don't listen to him! I have done good work here. I have full reports, hours of recordings. I will show that consciousness moves beyond our mediated space-time continuum. He disrespects the most important discovery in the history of science—can't you see that?'

'I'm here to sample and verify, Dr.Nowak. Unfortunately your data don't add up.' Dunwell slips her laptop into its leather case. 'I have another appointment. I must go.'

Having fired his salvo, Godd is now eager to disengage. 'We must leave the Doctor. She'll have a lot to do, winding all this up, making special arrangements for her laboratory pets.'

At the door he looks around the room, at its scuffed parquet, peeling veneer on the tabletop, fungal damp breaking through swirly brown/orange 1970s decor, and sniffs. 'You know, you can almost smell the odour of failure here.'

At the table Zofia sobs, head in hand. The future looks unworkable.

MONACO

Kevin had no idea of how long he had been sprawling across the rear seat of the battered Jaguar saloon, which he'd parked here on the hard shoulder when its thirsty V8 engine finally expired through lack of petrol. The codeine he'd taken to dull his raging headache had lulled him into a doze. Zoe, his young co-driver, must have gone in search of fuel, hoping to haggle for a can at one of the service areas that had not yet been cordoned off or barricaded.

It was mid day, the May Day sun at its zenith. He imagined her pacing along the baking concrete, baseball cap over her blonde hair, inhaling the traffic fumes like the bouquet of a rare vintage, soon to be dissipated forever.

Nevertheless cars still roared along the motorway. He was struck by the number of older vehicles, the automobiles of his 1950s childhood—dumpy Morris Oxfords, the flashy two tone Vauxhall Cresta favoured by salesmen and villains, a bulbous beige Austin Cambridge, old Fords in all shapes and models, even an elegant Armstrong-Siddley. Following them was a raucous motorcade of sports cars—Austin Healeys, MGs, Aston Martins. The silencers on their exhausts had obviously been removed, allowing them to snarl defiantly despite their impending obsolescence.

Perhaps their goggled drivers were all heading for one last gigantic vintage rally, a final celebration of hydrocarbon splendour.

He settled back on the worn leather upholstery and closed his eyes again. The non-stop throb of the sports cars reverberated through his skull. Hopefully Zoe would return soon with sandwiches and water, if not petrol. They needed to plot their next move, although planning was becoming increasingly problematic. The future was a mirage, trembling like heat waves over the high noon tarmac.

He was awakened by somebody knocking hard on the window. The roar of engines revving or backfiring was louder than ever.

'Excuse me, *monsieur*. We must remove this car. This area is for team members and accredited guests only. This is *parc fermé* or paddock, as you English call it.' A marshal of some kind, sporting a smart uniform and a waxed moustache, began opening his door. Kevin got out awkwardly, steadying himself against the car roof, and squinted up into a cloudless azure sky.

He was facing a hillside cityscape of blinding white buildings —tall apartment blocks with balconies, the ornate colonnades and porticos of hotels, the canopies of restaurants and casinos. Avenues lined with palm trees skirted a harbour where luxury yachts and cabin cruisers lay at anchor. He half shut his eyes against the glare and tried to block the incessant noise.

'Can I see your pass please, *monsieur*?' The official tapped him on the shoulder. He pretended to fumble in his pockets, the marshal waiting impatiently. A tow truck had arrived and a mechanic was already attaching a tow bar to the Jaguar. Then while he was trying to prolong the pantomime of a lost ticket, another official appeared and spoke urgently to his colleague. As far as Kevin could understand from his mediocre French there was some protocol issue about Prince Rainier and his entourage that required their immediate attention. The two men hurried away into the throng. The enclosure, packed with trucks and trailers, was swarming with photographers and journalists. Perhaps he could lose himself among them.

He pushed through the crowd towards the source of those ferocious internal combustion noises. Men in overalls were peering into the cockpits and engine compartments of classic Grand Prix cars that he recognised from 1950s boys' comics. He could see scarlet Maseratis and Ferraris, Vanwalls and BRMs in sober British green. Mechanics shouted back and forth as they checked rev counters, oil pressure and radiator levels, in final preparations for the start. The drivers wandered around casually in shirt sleeves as they strapped on their rudimentary helmets. A short balding man in his forties smiled as he autographed a programme for an overawed schoolboy.

'El Maestro never forgets the young fans,' said a bearded Brit at Kevin's elbow. 'My guess is he'll win, as usual. I could almost file my copy before the race starts.'

The bearded man, dapper in a sports jacket, introduced

himself as the motoring correspondent for one of the UK broadsheets. He was keen to share his enthusiasm with Kevin as he identified prominent figures in this gathering of bantering drivers and wide-eyed Vogue models. 'The fair-haired chap over there in the bow tie is Mike Hawthorne. He likes taking the rise out of Moss. Always trying to steal his crumpet. I expect they'll be really scrapping out there today. But we need to get to our seats. Don't worry, I have a spare. Come along...'

From his privileged vantage point in the Harbour grandstand, Kevin had a panoramic view of the fastest section of the track. Already with only a few laps completed there had been a spectacular incident. Stirling Moss, leading Peter Collins and Fangio, had slammed into the barriers of the chicane, forcing Collins to spin and hit the barricade on the harbour wall. The wily maestro had slipped deftly between them while Hawthorne slid into the wreck of Collins' Ferrari and lost a front wheel which bounced into the water. Kevin was relieved to see all three drivers were unharmed although obviously shaken as they limped away; but his new companion seemed disappointed. 'It's going to be a procession from now on. Old man Fangio's going to hold on to it all the way. I told you so...'

Soon Kevin was falling into a petrolhead trance, induced by the seemingly eternal recurrence of the same cars circulating lap after lap. Their exhausts ripped through the superheated air, which was saturated with fumes of scorched rubber and burnt oil, mingled with the odours of suntan lotion and sweat from the chattering crowds around him. To remain awake he needed distraction. While the journalist was holding forth to his press colleagues about tire changes and oil leaks Kevin borrowed his binoculars and started scanning the harbour and its fleet of expensive craft.

His gaze alighted on the largest vesse—Nemesis II— supposedly owned by the oil magnate Petros Oligakis. Its upper deck offered a wide vista of the waterfront track but its partying passengers were more intent on congregating around their saurian white suited host as waiters refilled their champagne

glasses. Fragments of cocktail jazz from a piano trio-drifted across on a faint breeze, in brief intervals between the din of passing cars.

Adjusting the focus of the binoculars Kevin recognised some celebrity guests—Elizabeth Taylor, David Niven, Noel Coward, Zsa Zsa Gabor and bikini clad Brigitte Bardot, who was reclining on a sun lounger, oblivious to the disdainful glance of Sophia Loren in her Dior chic. Others could only hover on the margins of this jet-set circle, like new starlet Mylene Demongeot, up-and-coming pop singer Sylvie Vartan, the young rocker Johnny Halliday and avant-garde icon Jacqueline Mayakovski, enigmatic in her sunglasses, who walked away to the rail and turned towards the sea.

As he watched the revelry Kevin felt increasingly uneasy as if some dark memory—or premonition—had been compressed deep in the strata of his consciousness and was about to bubble to the surface. There might be some terrible accident like a car ploughing into the spectators and exploding, as it had at Le Mans only two years previously. But his foreboding went further than that. The whole Roman circus on the deck of the yacht, its exuberant rite of conspicuous consumption, was somehow doomed. These absurd party people on the boat and the excited racegoers in the stand around him were all vulnerable, they were going to be consumed in a petrochemical rush to extinction on this overheated world which they were creating with their lethal emissions. For the sunlight that shone on Bardot's tanned shoulders and sparkled off the gleaming bodywork of the speeding cars might become a deadly radiance, a heat ray that would transform this coastal pleasure zone into a desert.

He handed the binoculars back to the journalist. 'It's no good. I've got to stop this—it's too dangerous!'

'What on earth are you talking about, old boy? There are still five laps to go. The man's out of his mind. Stop him, somebody!' Even as onlookers shouted Kevin was sprinting forward down the steps of the gangway to the flimsy barriers. Sidestepping a race marshal, he vaulted over the straw bales on to the track. 'I'm in the slipstream of time,' he yelled, but his words were lost in the roar of Fangio's Maserati as it lapped the tail-enders. Brooks, following in the Vanwall scowled and waved a fist, swerving to avoid contact.

Kevin started staggering through the heat haze back towards the tunnel leading onto the straight, in the hope of flagging down another driver and bringing the race to a halt but the field had now thinned down to six. Marshals and spectators were gesticulating furiously but he had to continue. Surely his desperate intervention would soon force them to abandon the race. The recurring adverts on the barriers, promoting Campari/Castrol/Dunlop/Campari into infinity were a blurred slideshow, like the flags waving over the stands, it was all spectacle in which his appearance was the most spectacular apparition of all...

Breathless, he had to stop in the dark tunnel mouth. The sound of rapid gear-shifting and squealing brakes still reverberated along its curved walls, pulsing through the pain and terror that filled his mind. He could only walk on into the darkness, cars hurtling past him like ghosts, until consciousness was lost.

Despite the heat Zoe broke into a run as soon as she saw the patrol car and ambulance parked next to the Jaguar. Its rear offside door was open. Two paramedics were loading a covered stretcher into their vehicle while a police officer was talking urgently on his phone. A WPC, a young British Asian woman with an anxious expression, hurried towards her.

'I'm afraid there's been an accident. Do you know him? Is he a friend or relative?'

'He's my colleague. We're journalists. Supposed to be covering the climate demo in London. But we ran out...' It was a numb mechanical response. She didn't know the right form of words at this point. She hadn't even succeeded in finding petrol. The only thing that made sense was to sit down on the barrier and twist off the cap of an energy drink.

The policeman came over. 'Hit-and-run, I'm afraid. But they have it on CCTV. It looks like he just walked out into the fast lane. Do you have any idea why he might have done something like that?'

The motorcade continued roaring past.

Also By The Terminal Press:

The J.G. Ballard Book 2013

Deep Ends: The J.G. Ballard Anthology 2014

Deep Ends: The J.G. Ballard Anthology 2015

Deep Ends: The J.G. Ballard Anthology 2016

Deep Ends: A Ballardian Anthology 2018

Deep Ends: A Ballardian Anthology 2019

Deep Ends: A Ballardian Anthology 2020

Deep Ends: A Ballardian Anthology 2021

Deep Ends: A Ballardian Anthology 2022

Deep Ends: A Ballardian Anthology 2023

Dominika Oramus - Grave New World: The Decline of the West in the Fiction of JG Ballard

Lawrence Russell - Radio Brazil

Lawrence Russell - Outlaw Academic

Lawrence Russell - Temple of the Two Moons

Don McKay - Gambari

Rick McGrath - Straight Man: Rock Star Interviews, Reviews & Photos from the 1970s Underground Press

Rick McGrath - The Disenchanted Forest

Rick McGrath (editor) - Unauthorised Departures